ONCE UPON A PROPOSAL

ALLISON LEIGH

SPECIAL EDITION

Published by Silhouette Books

America's Publisher of Contemporary Romance

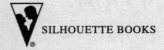

SILHOUETTE BOOKS

Recycling programs
for this product may
not exist in your area.

ISBN-13: 978-0-373-65560-1

ONCE UPON A PROPOSAL

Copyright © 2010 by Allison Lee Johnson

Printed in U.S.A.

"Gabe—" Bobbie's soft voice broke off.

He'd never before thought his thumb had a mind of its own, but evidently it did, brushing across the fullness of her lower lip.

Her gaze flickered. "Let's not forget what we're really doing here."

His left hand seemed damnably independent, too, sliding more firmly around her back, drawing her silk-draped curves even closer to him. "What I'm really doing," he murmured in her ear, "is trying not to kiss you right now."

Her head went back a little farther. Her long spiraling curls tickled his fingers pressing against her spine. "Really?"

"Don't be surprised," he reminded. "You started it." His lips closed over hers.

Dear Reader,

A few years ago, I had the privilege of sharing with three extraordinary authors the lives of Harrison Hunt and his four sons as he forced their hands into marriage... and happiness. The Hunt for Cinderella was the name of that rather magical series, and those other authors were Christine Flynn, Lois Faye Dyer and Patricia Kay.

Now, I'm lucky enough to visit Harry Hunt's world with them—*and you*—again!

This time Harry has set his sights on his dearest friend in the world, Cornelia Fairchild, and bringing marital bliss to her four daughters—Bobbie, Tommi, Frankie and Georgie. Naturally, in Harry-style, he goes about it in his oft-misguided way.

But once again, despite Harry's interfering ways, I'm happy to say that fairy-tale magic is alive and well.

Thank you for joining all of us to share a little more magic!

Allison Leigh

Books by Allison Leigh

Silhouette Special Edition

†*Stay...* #1170
†*The Rancher and the
    Redhead* #1212
†*A Wedding for Maggie* #1241
†*A Child for Christmas* #1290
Millionaire's Instant Baby #1312
†*Married to a Stranger* #1336
Mother in a Moment #1367
Her Unforgettable Fiancé #1381
The Princess and the Duke #1465
Montana Lawman #1497
Hard Choices #1561
Secretly Married #1591
Home on the Ranch #1633
The Truth About the Tycoon #1651
All He Ever Wanted #1664
The Tycoon's Marriage Bid #1707
A Montana Homecoming #1718
‡*Mergers & Matrimony* #1761

Just Friends? #1810
†*Sarah and the Sheriff* #1819
†*Wed in Wyoming* #1833
**A Cowboy Under Her Tree* #1869
††*The Bride and the Bargain* #1882
**The Boss's Christmas Proposal* #1940
§*Valentine's Fortune* #1951
†*A Weaver Wedding* #1965
†*A Weaver Baby* #2000
†*A Weaver Holiday Homecoming* #2015
‡‡*The Billionaire's Baby Plan* #2048
††*Once Upon a Proposal* #2078

†Men of the Double-C Ranch
**Montana Mavericks:
    Striking It Rich
‡Family Business
††The Hunt for Cinderella
*Back in Business
§Fortunes of Texas: Return to Red Rock
‡‡The Baby Chase

ALLISON LEIGH

There is a saying that you can never be too rich or too thin. Allison doesn't believe that, but she does believe that you can *never* have enough books! When her stories find a way into the hearts—and bookshelves—of others, Allison says she feels she's done something right. Making her home in Arizona with her husband, she enjoys hearing from her readers at Allison@allisonleigh.com or P.O. Box 40772, Mesa, AZ 85274-0772.

For my fellow hunters, Christine Flynn,
Lois Faye Dyer and Patricia Kay.
It's always a pleasure!

Prologue

"Corny, I promise you that I'm not meddling in the boys' affairs anymore." Harrison Hunt sat at his desk talking on the phone in an office high atop the HuntCom complex in Seattle. He no longer ran the computer juggernaut that had been a brainchild of his and his best friend, George Fairchild, a lifetime ago. Harry's eldest son, Grayson, ran the corporation now. But Harry still maintained this office at their headquarters.

He still kept his finger in a lot of pies—mostly because it pleased him to ruffle Gray's feathers. To keep the boy from becoming too much like his old man.

He didn't want his sons making the same mistakes he had. And while he hadn't been too popular with them a few years earlier when he'd forced their hands—into donning wedding rings—everything *had* turned out well all around. Even they managed to admit that.

Now.

"Don't lie to me, Harry," Cornelia Fairchild was saying. She was George's widow. More importantly to Harry, she was his oldest friend. "I had lunch with Amelia this afternoon."

Amelia. Gray's wife and, if truth be told, not at all the pushover that her sweet name and demeanor would suggest. Harry picked up one of the framed photographs on his desk of Gray and Amelia and their brood—larger than Harry had ever dared hope, considering his son and daughter-in-law were also raising Amelia's niece and nephews. "All I did was suggest that Gray wasn't getting any younger. If they want another baby, they ought to get cracking. That's true enough, isn't it?" He replaced the photograph among the others in his collection.

And there *was* a collection where, for much of his lifetime, there had been none at all.

"Coming from anyone but you, that might be a good enough assurance," Cornelia said warily. "Let your sons be, Harry. They've chosen their wives well. They're *happy*."

"Yes, they are," Harry agreed. Evidenced by their rapidly expanding families. He'd wanted grandchildren. And he'd gotten them.

At last he was happy. Wasn't he?

He decided to change tack, not wanting the conversation to end when it was the first time he'd heard her voice in nearly a week. "How are the girls?"

"Fine," Cornelia said immediately. "Georgie's enjoying working with Alex and all the traveling it includes. Frankie is busier than ever at the university. Tommi's working nonstop at that little bistro of hers."

"And Bobbie? She doesn't seem to be moping anymore about that idiot who broke up with her." He picked up the tall, insulated cup sitting on his desk pad. It was currently empty, but would be filled soon enough with a rich, caffeinated brew. Bobbie was Corny and George's youngest daughter. And *he* knew that he probably saw her more often than Corny did, since Bobbie personally delivered the high-octane drink to him twice a week.

"Thankfully. She's busy raising those dogs that she can barely afford to feed."

"Say the word, Corny, and none of your girls would have to work another day in their lives." It was an old argument. One he'd given up on ever winning.

Once George was gone and the financial plight he'd been hiding had come to light, Corny had insisted on cleaning up the mess all on her own. She'd flatly refused Harry's assistance in every single way. By anyone's standards, she'd managed to do well by her girls despite her diminished circumstances. Harry was as proud of each of them as he was of his own sons. But the most *he'd* ever been allowed to do for George's daughters was make an occasional gift to them. He'd still managed to spike Corny's guns a little, though. He'd given each of the girls a substantial monetary gift when they'd graduated from high school, as well as honorary seats on HuntCom's board. Seats they would have had eventually if their father hadn't secretly gambled away nearly every asset he'd possessed. Even in Harry's socially backward way, he'd wanted them to have options.

The girls, each of them, had been beyond thrilled.

Corny? Less so.

She hadn't spoken to him for a solid month.

"Don't even bring up the subject of money with me, Harrison Hunt," Corny said, sounding testy. "Anyway, the girls are all fine. Alone, of course, but I guess I shouldn't complain when that's generally of their own choosing."

"Living up to their mother's example," Harry pointed out, not for the first time. Cornelia had never remarried after George. She'd never been seriously involved with anyone again. As if she'd been determined to prove—after having had a marriage that turned out less perfect than it had seemed on the surface—that she needed only her daughters to be happy.

Even he could see the irony that it had taken him nearly two decades to recognize that particular point. But he'd been the one who could make a computer sing. It was George who'd had the gift of dealing with people, Cornelia in particular.

"I want my daughters to have fulfilling lives of *their* choosing," Cornelia returned pointedly. Harry's method where his fully grown sons had been concerned had been much more hands-on, considering he'd threatened to take away everything that mattered to them if they didn't get married and start families within the twelve months he'd allotted them. But he'd had good reason at the time, and even now he couldn't entirely regret the course he'd taken.

"You telling me you don't wish you could hold your own grandbabies in your arms before you die?"

Corny gave a short, muffled laugh. "Trust you, Harry, to remind me just how *old* I am."

He grinned, looking at the framed photograph from Gray and Amelia's wedding that sat in the center of all the rest. But it wasn't his son and new bride in the picture. It was Cornelia. Clothed in soft gold, slender and fair-haired and looking every bit as lovely as she had when she, George and Harry had been youngsters chasing around together. "What are friends for?"

She laughed again and his smile widened. It was there, even after they'd hung up. And a few minutes later, a familiar brunette with corkscrew hair peeked her head around his office door. She was holding a familiar-looking coffee cup.

How many times had he wanted to make Corny's dreams come true? Too many to count.

He waved his dearest friend's youngest daughter into his

office, his mind suddenly ticking. He'd gotten his boys onto the road of marital bliss, hadn't he?

Why not his dear Corny's girls?

His smile widened as Bobbie crossed the office toward him.

After all, what were friends for?

Chapter One

"Kiss me."

Gabriel Gannon stared at the petite bundle of curly-haired brunette energy standing in the doorway of his grandmother's carriage house. "Excuse—"

He didn't even get the rest of it out, as the girl—after a harried glance around him—grabbed his shoulders and yanked him down with an urgency that surprised him so much, he couldn't help but go with it.

Her mouth pressed against his. *"Kiss me,"* she muttered again, her lips moving against his as she twined her arms around his neck. "And for pity's sake, make it look good."

Look good? His brain was faintly aware of some insult there, but his hands were too busy being filled by the shapely body practically climbing up his. He had a vague recollection of the last time he'd kissed a woman. Some leggy blond architect he'd met in Colorado. Maybe he'd even taken her to bed.

Hell. Who could remember a minor detail like that when he had the taste of this little body-climber in his mouth, making him feel like the top of his head was about to blow right off?

His fingers flexed against her waist. Spread against her back, feeling the supple stretch of her spine through the soft fabric of her cherry-red shirt.

He'd seen her before, of course. She was his grandmother's new tenant, living in the old carriage house at the rear of Fiona Gannon's stately Seattle property.

But he damn sure had never figured on *this*.

His fingers flexed again and it took every speck of self-control he had not to run them down to her hips, to her rear, and drag her even tighter against him. Not to press her back against the opened front door—which he fleetingly remembered that he was there to fix—and really make it look good…

She made a soft sound, her mouth opening, her fingers sliding through his hair and her tongue dancing against his. Even through their shirts he could feel the soft push of her breasts; could feel, too, the way her heartbeat raced.

Or maybe that was his.

All he could think about was where in the hell was the nearest bed. Or couch. Or floor.

He took a step. Then another. Over the threshold of the doorway.

"Bobbie?" The deep voice came from behind them and an oath raced through Gabe's thoughts, but not past his lips, which were still fused to hers. "What's going on here?"

Gabe tore his mouth away, hauling in a deep gasp. His hands slowly—way too slowly—let go of his kissing bandit as he lowered her feet back to the floor. He caught a glimpse of startled gray eyes before her thick lashes fell and she looked around him at the man who'd interrupted them.

"Tim," she greeted, sounding as breathless as Gabe felt. "What are you doing here?"

Gabe couldn't even move away. For one thing, she had her arms wrapped around him in a maddening way that kept him trapped against her luscious curves. For another, he was none too anxious to face a strange guy while he felt strangled by jeans that had gone too tight.

He might as well be seventeen again, instead of the forty-one he really was, for the amount of self-control he seemed to have just then.

"I brought you these," the other guy—*Tim*—was saying, as he passed a bunch of sickly-sweet smelling roses between Gabe's shoulder and the doorjamb.

"Oh." Bobbie finally had to let go of Gabe's arm to take the flowers and he used the moment to take a step away. But her free hand frantically grasped his, holding him close with a strength that was surprising. "That's very sweet of you."

The fingernails digging into Gabe's palm didn't feel all that sweet. He looked down at the top of her head. It barely reached his shoulder. And behind the veil of the flowers that she was sniffing, the glance she flashed up at him looked decidedly panicked. Gabe's nerves tightened and this time it had nothing to do with wanting a woman for the first time in longer than he cared to admit.

He turned to face the intruder, casually sliding his arm around Bobbie's shoulders, tucking her neatly against his side.

Tim—who'd evidently been the reason why Gabe had needed to make anything look good on this particular October morning—didn't appear particularly threatening. Medium brown hair. Medium brown eyes. Creased khaki pants and a navy-blue crew-neck sweater. If anything, he looked like he belonged in one of those yuppie-courting store catalogs that

Gabe's daughter, Lisette, had suddenly begun showing an interest in.

But there was still no mistaking Bobbie's anxiety. So he curled his palm around the point of her shoulder in a possessive move that the other guy couldn't fail to notice. "Who is this, honey?"

"Tim." The other guy introduced himself before Bobbie could utter a word. "Tim Boering." He stuck his hand out, obviously not as put off by Gabe's arm around Bobbie as Gabe had hoped. "And *you?*"

"This is…is Gabriel Gannon," Bobbie finally spoke. She was probably trying to sound cheerful, but her musical voice mostly just sounded high-pitched and half-strangled. "Gabriel, Tim is a, um, a friend of Uncle Harry."

Gabe nodded, as if he had a single clue who in the hell her uncle was.

"Not just Mr. Hunt's friend, I hope." Tim shot Gabe a tight look before smiling winsomely at Bobbie. "You and I *did* spend a very memorable day together last weekend."

"Sightseeing," Bobbie put in quickly. "Uncle Harry asked me to show Tim around the city. He's just moved here from…" She trailed off, looking back at Tim with a question in her eyes.

"Minneapolis," Tim provided after the faintest of hesitations. He smiled a little deprecatingly, and Gabe supposed that if a woman liked that pretty-boy kind of guy, she'd probably lap it up. But in Gabe's estimation, Bobbie didn't seem the least bit thirsty. And the look Tim directed at Gabe was entirely competitive. "Are you an old friend of Bobbie's?"

Gabe smiled faintly, amused at the other guy's attempt to point out that he was plainly older than Tim. And Bobbie. He looked down at her. She was giving him another gray-eyed look of pleading. "Something like that," he murmured, his voice low. Intimate.

Her eyes widened slightly and that cool, panicky gray turned soft and warm. Then she blinked suddenly, looking away. She moistened her bow-shaped lips and color suffused her cheeks.

"I see," Tim said slowly. He tugged at his ear. "Bobbie, maybe I could call you later?"

Clearly, a lack of persistence wasn't one of Tim's faults.

Bobbie's mouth was opening and closing, as if she didn't know what to say. "I, well, I—"

Tim's gaze went from Bobbie to Gabe and back again. "I wasn't trying to poach. I just got the impression from Mr. Hunt that you weren't involved with anyone." He gave that toothy smile again. "I got that impression last weekend, too," he said to Bobbie.

If Gabe had to guess, he'd bet that Bobbie was wishing she could disappear into thin air as she hemmed around for something to say.

Gabe thought of the door he still had to fix for his grandmother before he could get out of there and pick up his kids for the day. At this rate, with Bobbie not getting rid of the guy she clearly wanted to get rid of, it was going to take more time than Gabe had.

"Blame that on me," he said smoothly. He nudged a finger beneath Bobbie's slightly pointed chin, and nudged it upward. "A misunderstanding, I'm afraid."

He lowered his head and pressed a kiss to the softly surprised O of her lips.

When he lifted his head, those gray eyes had a distinct silvery cast. He'd never seen anyone with eyes so expressively changeable. Fascinating. For a man with the time to explore it.

Which did *not* describe him.

He didn't even want to recognize the regret he felt as he brushed his thumb over the lips he'd just kissed, keeping up the act for young Tim. "But that's all worked out now, isn't it, sweetheart?"

She nodded hurriedly. "Mmm-hmm. For, um, for better or worse." Her cheeks were pinker than ever when she smiled brightly at Tim again.

"I see." Tim's expression tightened. "Well. Congratulations, then." He gave Gabe a terse nod and turned on his heel, striding back down the three porch steps to the stone walkway that led beyond the large main house and out to the hillside street.

Gabe leaned down again toward the riotous brown spirals covering her head. "I'm guessing you don't want to run and stop him?"

She let out a breathless sound and tilted her head to look up at him. "I…no." Her lips closed, softly pursed. They were pink and rosy. Lushly curved.

And now he knew they tasted sweeter than a summer strawberry.

It was all he could do not to take them again. He pressed his hand against the doorjamb above her head, realizing belatedly that he was still holding his hammer.

He didn't know whether to laugh at himself or curse. So he did neither. He straightened away from her and nodded toward the bouquet she was clutching. "Remind me never to give you roses. Lord knows what other innocent person you might attack."

She flushed and looked at the bouquet as if she'd forgotten all about it. "It's not the roses," she assured, running her hand over the perfectly pink blooms. "I love any sort of flower. And, I *am* sorry about, well, about all that."

He couldn't say that he was. "Getting kissed by a pretty girl isn't the worst thing that's ever happened to me."

Her lashes flew up and again he couldn't help but think

that she really did have the most distinctive eyes. And right now, they were as soft a gray as a mourning dove.

"Thank you." A dimple came and went in her smooth cheek. "I think."

"Just for future reference, though, if it wasn't the roses, what was so objectionable about the guy?"

"Boering wasn't just his last name." She gave a little huff, shaking her head and causing silky brown curls to dance around her shoulders. "And honestly, I never encouraged him. We spent a few hours visiting Pike Place and the Space Needle and I've been dodging his phone calls since."

"Ever think about just telling the guy you weren't interested?"

Her smooth forehead crinkled. "I tried!" She huffed a little at the look he gave her. "Honestly, I did. It's just not as easy as you make it sound. And I really didn't want to offend him. He's a friend of Uncle—"

"—Harry's," Gabe finished.

"Right."

"Well, I hope your Uncle Harry doesn't have too many friends like Boering that he sets you up with or you're—"

"No, no, no." Her curls danced some more. "Uncle Harry didn't set us up. He just happened to introduce us when I delivered some coffee to his office. He's not supposed to be drinking it, you see, but when he called me—" Her shoulders lifted.

"You couldn't say no to him, either." Gabe grinned a little.

Her lips curved, and that dimple flirted into view again. "I was just doing a favor. Really."

"Well." He tapped the doorjamb with the butt of his hammer. "Someday you can thank your Uncle Harry for me. Whoever he is."

This time her cheeks went even rosier than the velvety

flowers. Her eyes sparkled. "You're pretty gracious, considering everything."

"My grandmother would expect nothing less," he assured wryly.

"Right. And though Fiona has talked about you, we haven't ever been properly introduced." She tucked the roses under her arm and stuck out her hand. "I'm Bobbie Fairchild."

He took her palm in his. His hand practically swallowed her smaller one. "Gabe Gannon. It's nice to kiss you, Bobbie Fairchild."

She laughed. "I suppose I deserve the teasing."

If he teased long enough, maybe he could forget the taste of her. Which would be the smartest thing all around. For one thing, he had seriously more pressing issues going on than his dearth of a love life. For another, he figured Bobbie was one of the causes that his grandmother had taken under her wing. What other reason would Fiona have for suddenly renting out the carriage house the way she had?

It wasn't as if his grandmother needed the money. And it wasn't as if the carriage house was in such great shape. Structurally sound, maybe. But nobody had lived in the place for longer than Gabe could remember.

Which reminded him all over again about the door.

He lifted the hammer between them. "Fiona asked me to fix the door. It's been sticking?"

"If it's not sticking, then it's not locking properly." Bobbie was grateful to focus on something other than the way she'd virtually attacked the poor man. It seemed like hours since she'd yanked open the door at his knock, but she knew it really had only been a matter of minutes.

Only when she'd seen Tim Boering bearing down the walkway with determination in his step and roses in his hand, she'd simply panicked. No amount of hinting had been able to convince the man that she wasn't interested. And since there'd been six-plus feet of very manly man already standing on her porch, she'd impetuously decided to *show* Tim that she wasn't interested.

She just hadn't expected to find herself wrapped around a ticking bomb of sex appeal.

Her heart was still dancing around inside her chest.

And she realized that Gabriel Gannon, her sweet Fiona's oft talked-about grandson, was clearly waiting for her to say something.

The door. Right.

Her face felt hotter than ever as she backed up until she was out of the way of the opened door. "It stuck so badly the other day that I couldn't make it budge. I had to climb out the back window to get to work on time."

He had the decency not to laugh at that, though he didn't stifle his grin all that quickly. "Can only imagine. This old door's been warped since I was a kid." He was running his very long-fingered hand down the edge of the door but his gaze—impossibly blue—was on her. "You work with my grandmother, don't you?"

"At Golden Ability?" Fiona was the founder and long-time director of the small nonprofit canine assistance agency. "I'm just a volunteer for them. I actually work at Between the Bean. It's a coffee place downtown." Just the latest job in a long string of them, but she wasn't about to tell this man that. "Lots of, um, business people stop in there," she added even though she knew she was rambling. She just couldn't quite seem to help herself. Her brains still felt scrambled.

"What sort of volunteering do you do?" He straightened again from studying the door and moved around to the inside, giving her another whiff of the intoxicating scent that she'd noticed when she was kissing him.

"I'm a puppy raiser." She dumped the roses on the narrow entry table that was a general collecting ground for her mail and keys and puppy toys, effectively moving far enough away from him so that she wouldn't be in danger of accidentally drooling on him. He'd pulled a hefty screwdriver out of his back pocket and used it, along with the hammer, to tap out the hinges on the door. "Have been for about ten years." It was the longest she'd ever stuck with anything.

But then how could you not stick with raising golden retrievers that could—someday—become invaluable assistance dogs?

"For some reason, I had the impression that you were in the office with her." The hinges freed. He stuck the handles of his tools in the back pocket of his well-washed jeans, then wrapped his long, bare fingers around both sides of the weighty wooden door, lifting it right out of the door frame.

"Well, I've helped out now and then when she's short-staffed or something special's going on." She realized she was staring at the play of muscles beneath the short-sleeved white T-shirt he wore and quickly backed out of the way when he turned the door sideways to carry it out to the porch and down the steps where he leaned it against the iron railing. "What do you do with the door now?"

He dusted his hands together as he straightened. "I'll plane the edges. Shave off the warped parts," he translated when she gave him a blank look. "I've got the tools in my truck." He glanced at the sturdy watch that circled his wrist. "Won't take me long, and then your door will be back in business."

"Good grief." She darted down the steps, grabbing his wrist to look at his watch. "I forgot all about the time. I've got a class to get to." She raced back into the house, straight to the kitchen where she kept the puppies' kennel cages. Even when she was home, they preferred sleeping there, but when they heard her, the two fourteen-month-old dogs jumped to their feet and dashed out of the opened doors to race in circles around her. She snatched their leashes off the hook on the wall as well as the puppy jackets they wore when she took them out in public, and quickly clipped the leads onto their collars.

It took only a matter of seconds, yet the exuberant pups nearly pulled her after them, their paws scrambling as they ran across the hardwood floor to the front door. She had them back under control by the time they made it outside, though, and they waited obediently until she allowed them to go sniffing around the bushes that clustered against the foundation of the carriage house.

"Handsome dogs," Gabriel commented.

"They are." Glad for a reason to keep her eyes off of Gabriel's—well, *everything*—she crouched down and fondly scrubbed her fingers through Zeus's golden ruff. His eyes nearly rolled back in his head with pleasure. Archimedes wasn't so quick to finish his business before seeking out her attention, but that didn't surprise Bobbie. She'd gotten the pups just after they'd been weaned and even then, their personalities had been developing. "Zeus here is a little lover, plain and simple." She patted him on the back and nodded toward the other dog. "Archimedes there is the explorer."

And the explorer had moved from sniffing his way around the azaleas to the wooden door that was definitely not where he was used to it being.

He whined a little and trotted back to Bobbie, obviously ready for his share of petting when he sat his too-big-for-his-body paws right on her thigh, nearly knocking her over. She laughed and righted herself even as Gabriel's hand shot out to catch her arm.

"You okay?"

"Fine." Except that her arm was tingling all over again from his touch. "After all these years with puppies like these two, I'm pretty used to it. Have a collection of bruises most days," she added blithely as she moved away from him so she could breathe normally again and clipped on the leashes once more.

"Maybe you should try smaller dogs," he suggested dryly. "Ones that aren't half your size before they're even full-grown."

"Why?" She crouched down with the pups again, getting her face slathered with sloppy tongues while she deftly fastened their guide-puppy-in-training jackets on their backs. "What's a bruise or two when you get love like this?"

"There are bruises and then there are bruises."

She straightened again, unreasonably curious about the suddenly grim set of his lips, but he was already striding across the lawn toward the big dark blue pickup truck that was parked in the narrow drive in front of her cottage. A sign on the truck's door said *Gannon-Morris Ltd.*

"Come on, guys," she told the dogs as she followed him. "You'll be all right if I leave you?"

He reached into the bed of his truck and hefted out a large, red toolbox. "I think I can manage," he assured her solemnly.

She smiled. "Right." Of the two of them, there was no question that he would be the one in the "good at managing" column, whereas she was usually so *not*.

The corner of his lips twitched as he watched her just stand there. "Thought you had a class to get to."

"Criminy." Her face heated again. "I do." She lifted the dogs' leashes. "Obedience class, actually. It's held in the park at the end of the block, rain or shine." She glanced up at the partially cloudy sky. "So far, looks like we'll have a little shine. Thanks for fixing the door. And, thanks also for...you know—"

"Making it look good?" His gaze slid her way, and this time, the heat slowly oozed from her face and down her body into all manner of interesting places.

Zeus and Archimedes were tugging at their leashes. They knew they had a walk in store.

"Yes," she managed around her dry throat as her feet slowly followed their pull toward the street. "Making it look good." And then, before she could admit the painfully obvious—that he'd made it *feel* pretty darn good, too—she turned and followed the exuberant dogs.

At least trying to keep up with them gave her a safe excuse on which to blame her racing heart.

Chapter Two

"Fiona!" A few hours later, the door repairs nearly completed, Gabe entered the rear of his grandmother's house, going through the laundry room that—as far as he knew—had never once been used personally by his feisty, diminutive grandmother. That was something she'd always left for the "help"—individuals who, in Gabe's mother's opinion, were more in need of that particular quality than they were competent in providing it to Fiona.

"Fiona," he called again, gesturing for his son and daughter to go inside before he followed them with his heavy toolbox.

"I don't see why we can't stay home." Lisette continued her argument that had begun the moment she'd climbed in the passenger seat of his truck when he'd picked her up after her ballet lesson. "Twelve is old enough to babysit Todd."

"I don't need no babysitter," Todd returned acidly. He was two years younger than his sister, who never failed to remind him of her superior age. He headed straight to Fiona's oversize refrigerator and pulled open the door, sticking his rumpled blond head inside. "I'm hungry."

"You're always hungry," Lisette observed with a sniff that would have done her mother proud.

Gabe closed his hand around the back of her slender neck beneath the tight little knot she'd made of her pale-blond hair. "You should eat something, too," he told her, managing to contain the rest of his thought—that she was too thin.

"I'm not hungry." The response was predictable. Unfortunately, the way she shimmied out from his touch was predictable, too.

He stifled a sigh and set his toolbox on the floor in the kitchen. "Then help your brother. And if you wouldn't mind, fix a sandwich for me, too. I'm going to find your great-grandmother." Without waiting for an argument, he headed through a narrow hallway that led from the kitchen to his grandmother's office. But she wasn't behind the massive desk that had once belonged to Gabe's grandfather. Nor was she in the sunroom, fussing over her orchids and begonias. Where he did find his nearly 85-year-old grandmother was upstairs, standing on a six-foot ladder with a long-handled duster in her hand, trying to reach the lower arms of the enormous antique chandelier that hung suspended over the two-story foyer.

"Fiona," he said calmly from the foot of the stairs, because the last thing he wanted to do was startle her, even though he had to clench his hand over the carved newel top to keep from bolting up the stairs, "You told me you hired someone to clean the chandelier."

"Oh, I did." Leaning precariously over the handrail, she swiped the duster toward the chandelier. It groaned a little as it swayed slightly. "But Rosalie's poor husband was arrested."

"Ah." He began climbing the stairs. "The husband was the one you hired?"

"No, no." Fiona shook her head, and looked down, waving her duster at him as if he ought to know better. "Rosalie was the one I hired. But she obviously couldn't be *here* when she needed to be at her husband's side." She turned her attention back to the lofty chandelier.

"When was he arrested?" *And for what?*

"Oh, a week ago. I told Rosalie not to worry about a thing, financially or otherwise."

Gabe let out a slow sigh. Between his kids, who gave every impression of wanting him to disappear from their lives— again—and his grandmother, who was a soft-hearted target for every soul needing some sort of break, he had definitely been learning the fine art of keeping his patience.

He reached the top of the stairs and turned along the landing. "Grandma," he said mildly, "why not hire someone else?" He knew from long habit that there was no point in trying to convince Fiona that she didn't need to save everyone she met. "Or wait for me to get here and save your money altogether? You knew I'd be here today." He made it to the ladder and reached up, closing his hands around her waist and lifting her right off the ladder.

"Gabriel—" she swatted at him with the duster, giving him a face full of dust "—put me down this instant."

"That's what I'm—" he let out a huge sneeze "—doing." He set her well away from the ladder. And kept himself between her and it. He sneezed again, and swiped his hand down his face. "How much dust was *up* there?"

"A lot," Fiona said tartly. "Which is why it needed to be done." She propped her narrow hands on her skinny hips and eyed him with no small amount of relish when he sneezed a third time. "That's what you get for interrupting me."

He snatched the wooden handle out of her hand before she could brandish the feathery thing in his face again. "I'll finish it."

"Don't be ridiculous." She grabbed the handle right back, proof that age hadn't slowed her much at all. "I thought you had Lisette and Todd this afternoon?"

"I do. And they're downstairs raiding your kitchen as we speak."

Fiona's eyes lit up. "They're here, then? That's wonderful. For how long?"

"Not long enough." He grimaced. "I tried to get Stephanie to let me keep them overnight, but—" He shook his head.

Fiona's gave a frowning sniff. "As usual, she wants to make things as difficult for you as she possibly can."

Gabe could have denied it, but what would have been the point? His grandmother knew as well as anyone in the family just how little love was lost between him and his former wife. Fiona was about the only one, though, who didn't blame him for it.

Now, she patted him on the arm and waved at the ladder. "It really needs to be cleaned up before that dreadful birthday party your mother is insisting on next weekend."

"Would that be dreadful because it is *your* birthday? Or because Astrid is throwing it?" Not only did his mother like to control everything, but she was far from a devoted daughter-in-law. Any party his mom threw would be about appearances—hers. Sweet and loving, she was not.

Fiona gave him a look. "Take your pick. Were you able to fix Bobbie's door for her earlier?"

She didn't wait around for an answer, but tugged at the sleeves of her sweater as she wandered along the long landing, straightening the frames of the portraits hanging there. Three generations of Gannons and not a blue-collar guy like Gabe among them.

"Yeah." He climbed the ladder and began finishing the job his grandmother had begun. "I'm going to replace the lock set, though, before I leave today. She said she's been having problems with that, too."

"So you saw her, then."

"I saw her." An understatement if there ever was one.

"What did you think of her?" Fiona stopped in front of the portrait of her husband, cocking her white head as she nudged one corner of the frame. "A dear girl."

That "girl" had felt like she was all woman when she'd been filling his arms. "Seemed friendly enough," he offered. Another understatement. He realized he was grinning like some damn fool at the crystal prisms above his head. "She was taking her dogs out to some class."

"She teaches it, actually. When it comes to the dogs, she'll do most anything." Evidently satisfied with the portraits, Fiona moved to the top of the stairs. "That's good enough, darling. If your mother wants to get up on a ladder to inspect the thing, she's welcome to do so." She shook her head. "As if I need some darn party to remind me just how old I am." She started down the steps with an ease that belied her age. "Will that lock thing take you long enough that I can purloin your children for an hour or so?"

He eyed her from his perch atop the ladder. "What are you planning?"

She waved her hand at him. "Nothing for you to worry yourself about."

He made a face. "The last time you told me that, I ended up with two hamsters that had to live with me," he reminded her. And those two hamsters had quickly multiplied...fertile devils that they were. It had taken him nearly three months to find homes that had been satisfactory to his kids.

"We won't come back with anything that breathes," she assured, disappearing down the hallway where he could hear her cheerfully greeting his kids.

He shook his head and climbed off the ladder. Just because

whatever it was didn't breathe didn't necessarily mean it would be welcome. But he wasn't going to complain.

Neither Todd nor Lisette was chomping at the bit to spend time with their old man, but they *did* enjoy their great-grandmother and for that, Gabe could be grateful. He folded up the ladder and carried it and the duster downstairs, stowing them both in the cluttered utility closet. Fiona and the kids were still in the kitchen when he got there. Not surprisingly, there was no sandwich waiting for him and the way their chattering clammed up the second they spotted him wasn't exactly comforting. "No new pets," he warned again, giving each of them—including Fiona—a stern look before he picked up his toolbox and headed for the door. "I'll be done in an hour and maybe, *maybe,* I'll take you to the movies afterward. Okay?"

One thing Gabe knew was that Stephanie and Ethan rarely let the kids go to a movie theater. And maybe he shouldn't be proud of offering them this particular treat, but sometimes a man had to pick his battles. He'd had an ongoing one with Stephanie when it came to the children since they'd split up eight years earlier, but now the stakes had escalated.

And sometimes he simply needed to see a smile on his kids' faces. One that was directed at him.

Right now, both Lisette and Todd were looking surprised and pleased. "Check the newspaper for the movie times," he added. "And nothing rated R."

"Dad." Lisette rolled her dark blue eyes—the only feature she'd inherited from him. "Don't be lame."

"Would you rather I said to find something rated G?"

She rolled her eyes again, but shook her head. "I'm not going to the theater in my leotard, though. Somebody might see me."

"You'll have time to change," he promised, smiling faintly.

"Nobody cares what you look like anyway," Todd added,

ever the supportive little brother. "'Specially not *Jeffrey* Russell," he goaded.

"Shut up." Lisette rounded on him, lifting her fist. "Or you'll—"

"Make me change my mind about the movie altogether," Gabe warned.

Lisette's hand slowly dropped, though she gave Todd a killing glare. One that he returned, complete with crossed eyes.

Fiona quickly nudged Gabe out the door. "Go on. Finish Bobbie's door. Everything's fine here."

He wouldn't go so far as to say *fine,* but they were pretty much standard. The only thing Lisette and Todd could unequivocally agree on was their mutual annoyance with each another.

That at least was something that Gabe understood. He'd grown up with two older brothers, and a day hadn't passed when they hadn't been squabbling about something. But as he crossed the expanse of lawn leading toward the carriage house, he hoped to hell that he could keep Lisette and Todd from growing up to be as distant from one another as he was now from Liam and Paul.

When he reached the carriage house, he could hear dogs barking inside. Evidently the obedience class was over.

He knocked and a moment later Bobbie pulled open the door, a phone tucked between her ear and her shoulder and her other hand latched onto Zeus's collar. Her dark brown hair hung in dozens of long spirals around her shoulders. "Hey," she mouthed. "Door works great." She swung it back and forth.

He held up the new lock set. "It'll just take a few minutes."

Her mother was chattering in her ear, but Bobbie didn't really hear her. "You're replacing the lock, too?"

Gabe's deep blue eyes crinkled at the corners. "Neighborhood like this, a pretty woman should be able to lock her door securely."

She couldn't help but laugh at that. Fiona Gannon's neighborhood wasn't exactly one prone to petty crime and break-ins. It was far too well-bred.

"Bobbie?" Her mother's voice had sharpened in her ear. "Are you listening at *all?*"

"Sorry, Mom. Can you hold on for just a second?" She didn't wait for an answer, but tucked the receiver under her arm and focused on her landlady's handsome grandson again. Not exactly a hardship. The man was eye candy in a serious way. And he'd taken note when she'd mentioned the troublesome lock. "You didn't need to replace it," she told him now. "I figured it just needed a squirt of oil or something."

"It needs replacing," he assured. "The tumblers are worn down to nothing."

"Well." She moistened her lips, very aware of the fact that she was practically staring at him. "That's really nice of you. Thanks."

"We at Gannon-Morris are all about full service."

Warmth zipped through her. "I'll bet."

"Bobbie? RobertaNicoleFairchild—"

She realized the faint voice was coming from the forgotten telephone tucked beneath her arm and felt a new flush—this one entirely from embarrassment—flood her cheeks. "Excuse me," she told Gabe and quickly turned away, pulling Zeus with her into the kitchen. She pointed, and he trotted into the kennel cage alongside Archimedes, turned a few circles and plopped down with a noisy breath. "Sorry, Mom. I wasn't ignoring you." She stuck the phone back to her ear, keeping her voice low. "I just had someone at my door."

She heard her mother give a faint sigh. "And you still haven't answered me. Why did I have to learn from Harry, of all people, that my own daughter is engaged again? You can imagine what he thought when it was clear I had no idea what he was talking about." Cornelia Fairchild's voice rose slightly, a true indicator that she was genuinely perturbed.

If there was one person in the family to perturb the normally unflappable, elegant woman, Bobbie knew it was she, Cornelia's youngest daughter. The one who was entirely flappable. And decidedly *in*elegant.

A pain was beginning to form between her eyebrows. "I'm not—" she broke off, lowering her voice again. "I'm not engaged," she said in a half-whisper.

"Then why is Harry so certain that you are?"

There could be only one reason, Bobbie knew, though she really couldn't fathom why Tim Boering would have immediately trotted out the story for her honorary uncle. Only a few hours had passed since then, for heaven's sake. "It's just a misunderstanding," she assured. She lifted the roses out of the plastic pitcher that she'd stuck them in, and dumped them in the trash.

"Harry sounded perfectly clear to me, Bobbie. He said you and this Gabriel person were engaged!"

"Honestly, Mom—" her voice rose despite herself "—do you *really* think I would be seriously involved with someone and not tell you?"

Cornelia's silence was telling and Bobbie pressed a finger to that pain over her nose. Yes, over the years, there had been a few things she hadn't told her mother. Mostly because she knew it would just make Cornelia worry. And Bobbie had already caused her mother enough worry to last a lifetime.

"I promise you," she said more quietly, "I am *not* engaged." Particularly not to the eminently kissable man who was working on her door not twenty feet away from her, probably overhearing every word, even though she was nearly whispering.

"It's not the idea of you being engaged that alarms me, Bobbie," Cornelia countered smoothly. "It was the fact that I thought you hadn't *told* me first. I would be delighted to think that one of my daughters is finally settling down."

The pain went from a dull ache to a sharp throb. "You mean that *I* was finally settling down." Sticking with something. Anything.

"Don't put words in my mouth, darling. That's not what I meant at all."

Bobbie paced the confines of the small kitchen. She was twenty-seven years old and kept telling herself that she should be past the need for her mother's approval.

But saying it and feeling it were two very different things.

"I'm not even dating anyone, Mom. I haven't since—" She broke off. There was no need to finish. Her mother knew what she was referring to, and Bobbie had no desire for Gabe to overhear that her love life had as much altitude as Death Valley. A state of reality since the beginning of the year, ever since the man she'd been in love with—Lawrence McKay—had thrown her over for an entirely more suitable woman to stand at his side while he took the political scene by storm. A woman whose hair didn't look like she'd stuck her finger in an electric socket and who didn't need to stand on a stool just to reach the shelves in her own kitchen cabinets. A woman who was cool and elegant and who always had the right words for any situation.

A woman just like Bobbie's mother. Or her sisters, for that matter.

She pinched the bridge of her nose. Zeus started whining. She heard her mother sigh again. Faintly.

"All right. I'll just have to call Harry and correct his misinformation."

"I'll call him if you want me to," Bobbie offered. Her

honorary uncle was an eccentric one, but she had a soft spot for the man anyway. After Bobbie's father died when she was little, Harrison Hunt had been one of the few males left in her life. Whether it was the fact that he'd been childhood friends with George and Cornelia, or the fact that George had later married Cornelia, or even that George had been in business with Harry, once Bobbie's father had gone, Harry had tried—in his oft-awkward way—to do his best by the Fairchild family. The man was insanely brilliant but had— according to some—a computer chip like those that had made him rich for a heart. And given the way he'd treated his own sons for most of their lives, it wasn't an entirely inaccurate accusation. But to Bobbie, he was just her rather odd-duck Uncle Harry. And being an odd duck herself, maybe that's why she felt a kinship to him.

"I know he enjoys hearing from you," Cornelia was saying. "Particularly since you sneak him those coffees he loves—and don't bother denying it, darling. I've been onto this collusion between the two of you since you went back to work at that little coffee house after you and Lawrence ended things. But I'm having lunch with Harry tomorrow, anyway, so I'll set him straight. Now. Do you need grocery money? What about gas for the car?"

Bobbie couldn't prevent a groaning laugh. "No, Mom. I don't need grocery money or gas! I do have a job, remember? I can afford to take care of myself."

"Yes, I know you have a job. And I also can guess just how much of your income you're spending on those dogs of yours. If I came over there right this moment and looked in your pantry, would I actually see food for *you* and not just enormous bags of dog food?"

"Yes, you would." She childishly crossed her fingers as she envisioned the virtual void behind the pantry door.

Cornelia made a soft sound that Bobbie translated as

disbelief. But her mother didn't pursue the matter. Maybe because she herself was the most independent woman that Bobbie knew. And she'd raised her daughters to be the same.

"Besides," Bobbie added, "I'm helping Tommi out this week at the bistro." She smiled, thinking of her older sister's penchant for feeding the world through her charming Corner Bistro in downtown Seattle. "So you know I'll be eating well there, at least." As far as Bobbie was concerned, Tommi was the best chef in town. What her sister could do in the kitchen was simply magical.

"That's something, I suppose," Cornelia allowed. "All right, then. You're *certain* there isn't anything going on in your life that I should know about?"

The sound of a hammer filled the small cottage, a needless reminder of the man on the other side of the very thin kitchen wall. "Positive." She had no intention of informing her mother that she'd practically accosted Gabriel Gannon in order to avoid her uncle's young friend. "Tell Uncle Harry hello for me when you see him tomorrow. Love you."

She barely waited to hear her mother return the sentiment before she hung up the phone.

Alongside his sleeping companion, Zeus cocked his golden head, watching her as if he knew exactly how many times she'd skirted the facts with her mother. She rubbed her hand over his silky head and tossed him the hard rubber bone he liked to chew. Then she ran her hands over her hair in a vain attempt to smooth it down, straightened the hem of her long-sleeved T-shirt around her hips, and went back out into the living room.

Gabriel was crouched down next to the open door, working on the latch and the lock, his muscular thighs bulging against his worn jeans. She sucked in a careful breath and managed a smile when his vivid gaze turned toward her. "Your mother, I take it?"

Feeling more like a schoolgirl than a grown woman, she nodded and willed herself not to blush.

"Sounds like news traveled fast."

Forget staving off the blush. She felt heat plow up her neck into her face. "Yeah." She rubbed her palms down her thighs. "Guess you heard."

"I tried not to." He looked amused as he focused again on the new lock he was installing. "But it's kind of a small space."

And feeling smaller by the second. "I'm sorry."

"For what?"

She lifted her shoulders. "Getting your name involved in all this."

"Like you said, it's just a misunderstanding. No sweat." He finished tightening a screw, twisted the door latch a few times and pushed to his feet. "And I know how mothers can be." He shut the door and turned the lock. It latched with a soft, decisive click. He looked down at her. "Ought to keep you snug as a bug in here now."

She was feeling quite snug, with the door shutting out the world and shutting *him* in. "I, um, should pay you for the lock."

"Not necessary." He shook his head and smoothly unlocked and opened the door again, letting in a rush of cool, damp air. "Fiona has a long list of things she wants fixed or replaced over here. One lock set isn't going to make a difference." He leaned over to fit his tools back into the tool box and his shirt stretched tightly across his back.

She quickly looked past the tantalizing play of muscles beneath white cotton, through the open door, grateful for the waft of fresh air. "I told Fiona she didn't have to fix anything. Except for the door sticking, everything is fine over here." And the rent was ridiculously low.

"Don't say that," he drawled. "Business down the way it is, I need all the work I can get."

Horrified, she opened her mouth, not certain what to say.

But he was giving her that crooked grin again. The one that sent strange little squiggles of excitement through her belly. "I'm kidding. Playing Mr. Fix-it for my grandmother isn't exactly a hardship and after all the hours I'm spending in the office these days, it helps keep me from forgetting where I started." He lifted the toolbox. "If it stays dry enough tomorrow, I'll get new shingles up on your roof. Otherwise it'll be the floor in your bathroom."

She was almost afraid that he'd ask to see it, and considering the lingerie that was hanging over the shower rod to dry, she really wanted to avoid that. "When Fiona said she'd send someone to fix the door, I didn't expect it to be you." In fact, her elderly friend had implied it would be someone *employed* by her grandson's construction firm. Not her grandson himself. From what she'd heard over the years from Fiona about her wealthy family, very few of them were the hands-on type. Doctors and lawyers. Administrators.

Only her grandson had bucked the old money and professional tradition and gone into construction. And now he had branches in Colorado and Texas as well as Washington State. All details courtesy of Fiona, of course. The woman didn't try to hide how proud she was of him.

"Afraid you're stuck with me," he said. "I've got everyone on my payroll working at the moment."

"That's good, though, right?" She knew how construction had taken a terrible hit in this economy. "A sign of better things?"

He looked out the door. "I'm hoping so."

Something in his voice caught at her, but she didn't have time to examine it, because footsteps pounded on the walkway outside and a moment later, two kids—a boy and a girl—practically skidded to a stop on her porch.

"We picked the movie," the tousle-haired boy said. "But it starts in twenty minutes."

"And I still have to change," the girl said. She was wearing a black leotard with a short, filmy skirt over pale-pink tights, her hair fastened in a classic knot at the back of her blond head.

"Right." Gabriel looked back at Bobbie. "But first say hello to Ms. Fairchild. This is my daughter, Lisette. And my son, Todd."

Of course. He had children. Fiona had mentioned them. As well as the fact that their father was doing his best to regain partial custody of them. "It's nice to meet you," she greeted. "But call me Bobbie. Please."

Both of the youngsters had their father's brilliant blue eyes, but that was all. His hair was as dark a brown as theirs was pale blond. Even their features were different, not as sharply drawn, though she supposed that could just be the difference between youth and maturity.

"Hi." Todd was the first to speak. "You have the curliest hair I ever seen."

"Todd," Lisette groaned, rolling her eyes.

"Well she *does*," he defended innocently.

Bobbie laughed. "It is pretty curly," she admitted. "I always wanted smooth, blond hair, just like your sister's."

Lisette's hand flew up to her bun, looking away shyly. "Mother won't let me cut it," she said.

"All right," Gabe inserted. "Enough talk of hair. Go get in the truck. I'll be there in a sec." He gave Bobbie that smile again. "A movie awaits."

"Enjoy." She reached for the door. "Wait. Is there a new key for the lock?"

He shook his head. "It's already keyed to match the old one."

She realized she was staring at his lips again. "Thanks. Yet again." She smiled, feeling strangely awkward. As if he could read her mind.

And maybe he could, because his smile widened slightly. "The pleasure was all mine."

Then he turned and went after his kids.

And for the second time that day, Gabriel Gannon left Bobbie with a racing heart.

Chapter Three

"*I'll have a medium iced mocha with extra cream and a large iced tea.*"

Bobbie's head whipped up from the inventory sheet she was completing when she recognized the voice on the other side of the counter. She left the paperwork on the tiny desk in the minuscule office and peered around the doorway.

Yes. It *was* Gabriel, looking much more polished and no less devastating in a white button-down shirt and black trousers than when he'd been wearing worn jeans and a T-shirt while muscling her front door out of its frame. Before he could spot her, she pulled her head back into the office like some nervous turtle retreating into its shell.

What was he doing here?

She saw herself in the little mirror that Holly, the manager of Between the Bean, kept hanging on the wall in her office. At least her hair was contained in a ponytail. More or less.

And she'd put on some makeup that morning before leaving the house.

Then she rolled her eyes at herself. It wasn't as if he'd come to the coffee shop to see *her*. All he'd done was order a drink for himself and his son.

Chewing the inside of her lip, she tilted her head again, sliding centimeters forward until she could see once more around the doorway.

"Bobbie?"

She straightened like a shot when his gaze fastened on her across the array of pastries and oversized cookies displayed above the counter. "Gabriel." She stepped out of the office, moving to the counter beside Doreen, who was preparing his order. "What a surprise." She smiled at the boy standing at his side who was avidly eyeing an enormous chocolate-chip cookie. "Hello, Todd." The boy was dressed in tan pants and a navy-blue polo shirt—clearly a school uniform.

The boy grunted a greeting in return. "Can I have a cookie?" he asked his father.

"Your mother will have enough of a fit when she finds out we stopped and got you a mocha." Gabe handed the boy the change that Doreen had given him and pointed at the arrangement of chairs around a vintage video game in one corner of the small coffee shop. "You can play that game over there, though."

Evidently it was a satisfactory substitution, because Todd scooped up the coins and ambled over to the empty corner. Within seconds, the electronic beeps and chimes of the game began accompanying the funky music that was already playing through the sound system. Bobbie watched Doreen squirt a generous helping of whipped cream on top of the iced mocha drink. "For the boy?" Doreen asked and when Gabe nodded, she slid his tall glass of tea toward him then carried the mocha around the counter to deliver it to Todd.

Bobbie's curiosity couldn't be contained, no matter how it made her look. And she couldn't imagine what had brought him to this area of downtown. "What are you doing here?"

Doctoring his tea with sugar—the real stuff—he slanted a glance at her through lashes that were ridiculously thick. "Getting a drink?"

"Obviously." She toyed with the narrow tie of her dark-brown apron. Since the day that he'd worked on her door, she hadn't seen him again, though she'd come home last night after working a late shift for Tommi at the bistro to find that the cracked linoleum in her minuscule bathroom had been replaced by silky-smooth travertine. He'd left a note tucked against the mirror that he'd be back soon to finish it up. "I've just never seen you in here before." She would have definitely remembered him, even *before* the kissing attack.

"I had to pick up Todd from school. He attends Brandlebury Academy."

It was a prestigious private school. She drove by its ivy-covered walls every day on her way to the coffee shop. And *it* most certainly was in the area.

Which meant that Gabe hadn't been seeking her out, after all.

She didn't like acknowledging the disappointment that swept through her, so she smiled more brightly than ever. "Some of Uncle Harry's older grandchildren attend Brandlebury," she said. "I hear it's an excellent school."

Gabe's dark brows pulled together for a moment. "For the cost, it ought to be. Wouldn't those grandchildren be your cousins?"

"Yes, I guess they would be. But Harry's not really my uncle. He's a family friend."

Doreen snorted softly as she returned to the counter and picked up the rag she'd been using to polish the glass counters.

"And wouldn't we all like to have Harrison Hunt as a family friend?"

Gabe gave Bobbie a startled look. "Harrison *Hunt* is your Uncle Harry?"

Bobbie gave Doreen an annoyed glare that didn't faze her coworker in the least, though she fortunately moved out from behind the counter and over to the windows that overlooked the sidewalk and began polishing them. Doreen knew about Harry only because of the coffee that Bobbie delivered to him several times a week. She also knew that the relationship wasn't one that Bobbie necessarily wanted to advertise.

People expected things from you—things you couldn't provide—when they learned you were all but family to one of the wealthiest men in the country. Even people you thought you could trust.

She blocked off the thought and focused on Gabe, who was still staring at her with surprise. "Yes," she admitted shortly. "Harrison Hunt is my uncle Harry."

"Fiona never mentioned that," Gabe murmured.

"Why would she? It's not as if Uncle Harry—or Hunt-Com—has anything to do with Fiona's agency."

Gabe still looked a little bemused. "Considering how often Fiona *does* talk about you, I'm surprised it didn't come up even just in passing."

"Fiona talks to you about me?" Now it was her turn to be surprised.

"You're one of her favorite people," Gabe said. "Yeah, she talks about you quite a bit." He didn't use a straw to drink his tea, but lifted the cup to his lips instead. "It's good."

They sold gallons of the brew every day, so she'd assumed it was passably drinkable. "Fiona is one of my favorite people, too," she said truthfully.

He looked at her over the cup, his eyes crinkling at the corners. "Then we have something in common."

She suddenly felt a little breathless and she quickly began reorganizing the collection of stirrers and coffee cup lids sitting on the counter. "Do you always pick up your son from school?"

The smile lines around his eyes disappeared so instantly that she almost wondered if she'd imagined them in the first place. "No."

That was all. Just *no*. Which left her feeling like she'd awkwardly put her foot in her mouth, without even knowing why. Nothing new there. Saying the wrong thing was her specialty. Always had been.

She moistened her lips and pulled a fresh sleeve of small coffee lids from beneath the counter. "Thanks for the work you did in the bathroom. The tile looks great."

"I still need to grout it. I'll come by Saturday morning if that works for you."

"Sure."

"Dad." Todd had left the video game and stopped next to Gabe. "Can I get more whipped cream?" He held up his cup.

"One helping was enough."

The boy's brows drew together, and Bobbie realized that Gabe's son did share more than just the color of his father's eyes. He had the same expressions. "It's, um, no big deal," Bobbie offered softly. She pulled the can from its refrigerated slot behind her and held it up.

Gabe's gaze went from Bobbie to his son and back again. "Okay." He took Todd's cup and handed it over to Bobbie. "But just this once."

Todd's expression went straight to shock, giving Bobbie the sense that Gabe didn't often give in once he'd made a decision. She added the extra helping of cream and slid the drink back to Gabe, wishing that her interest in the man wasn't increasing with every encounter they had. She had no desire to change the zero status of her love life. Not when she still felt the bruises from Lawrence's defection.

"What do you say?" Gabe prompted his son and the boy gave Bobbie a brilliant, grinning "thanks," before carrying his drink with him back to the video game.

Doreen had disappeared into the back storeroom and the rest of the shop was still unoccupied. Yet there was no earthly reason for Bobbie to feel as if she and Gabe were suddenly the last two people on earth. Alone, together.

She couldn't help but smile a little at her own nonsensical thought.

"What?"

She shook her head. "Nothing." She pushed the sleeve of lids back beneath the counter—the holders were already full. She pushed her hands into the patch pockets of her apron to keep from fidgeting. He had his iced tea. His son had his mocha with extra, *extra* cream. So why wasn't he going on his way? "Is there anything else I can get for you?"

It wasn't often that Gabe found himself struggling for words. Unfortunately, that day, it had happened twice. The first time had been when he'd heard his attorney's thoroughly crazy and unwelcome advice that he find himself a wife—and fast. And the second time—now—when he was faced with the young woman he realized could possibly help him get around the attorney.

He glanced over his shoulder. Todd was completely occupied with the game in the corner. He looked back at Bobbie, who was watching him with those changeable gray eyes of hers. "Would you like to have dinner tonight?"

Her lips parted softly. "I…can't. I'm sorry." Her silky lashes swept down for a moment. "I'm helping to cover a shift at my sister's bistro this week." She looked up at him again and a hint of pink crept into her cheeks. "Maybe another time?"

He couldn't afford to wait a week. "What time are you finished at the bistro?"

"Between ten and eleven, usually."

"Where's it located? I could give you a lift home."

Her eyes narrowed a little. Her voice cooled—entering the same territory it had been in when she was dealing with her wannabe suitor, Tim. "I have a car."

"This is coming out wrong," he admitted, exhaling. "I'm not trying to sound like a stalker."

She shifted and placed her palms flat on the gleaming glass countertop. Her fingers were long and slender, the nails cut short and unvarnished. The only jewelry she wore was a narrow watch with an equally narrow leather band. "Why don't you tell me what *this* is, then?"

"There's something I'd like to talk to you about. Somewhere a little more private."

"Is Fiona all right?"

"Yeah," he assured quickly. "Fine as always. This doesn't concern her at all." He lowered his voice. "It's about my children, actually."

The wariness didn't entirely leave her face. She looked over at Todd. "What about them? I suppose Fiona told you that I had a job as a nanny a few years ago, but—"

"No, actually, she hasn't. But child care's not the kind of help I'm looking for."

"Then what—"

"I'll tell you everything, just not here. Not now."

Her gaze dropped to the counter, to his hand, which had covered hers. Then she looked up again, her shoulder moving in a faint shrug beneath the gleaming brown ringlets spilling over it. "All right." She slipped her hands from beneath his and tucked them back in her apron pockets. "If it can't wait until you come to work on the floor this weekend, you can meet me at Tommi's place. The Corner Bistro." She told him where it was located. "If you want the best meal you've ever had, then come early before she shuts down the kitchen."

He wasn't worried about finding a good meal. He was worried about losing his children for good. "Thanks. I'll see you tonight."

Then, before he could second-guess what he was even contemplating, he peeled Todd away from the game, and quickly left.

"You wanted a private place to talk." Bobbie untied the red apron from her hips and neatly folded it before sitting down across from Gabe. "You've got it."

All of the other tables in her sister's small bistro had been emptied. The other servers had finished their duties and departed for the evening. Even Tommi—after sending ping-ponging looks of concern between Bobbie and the lone man occupying a table near the wine bar—had finished her tasks in the kitchen and gone to her apartment upstairs, leaving Bobbie the responsibility of locking the back door after herself when she left.

"Want a glass?" He held up the wine bottle that was sitting in the center of the table.

Drinking one of her sister's very excellent wines was one thing. Drinking that wine while alone with the man she couldn't seem to stop thinking about was another. She shook her head. "No, thank you."

He refilled his own glass. His dishes had been cleared away—by Bobbie herself, who'd prayed all evening that she wouldn't do something stupid, like spill his entree in his lap. It was one prayer that she'd been granted, at least. "Only thing better than a good wine is a cold beer. And you're right about the food," he offered now. "Your sister is a remarkable chef."

"I'll tell her you said so." She was immensely proud of her

sister's accomplishment where the Bistro was concerned. But she didn't want to talk about Tommi. "So, what is it, exactly, that you wanted to talk to me about?"

He took a sip of his wine. He'd abandoned the fine slacks and shirt of that afternoon and replaced them with black jeans and a thickly woven black sweater with the sleeves shoved up his forearms. The sturdy watch circling his sinewy wrist gleamed in the soft light coming from the wine bar as he set the glass down again, and she had to swallow a little. He was *so* incredibly masculine.

"My ex-wife's husband is a corporate lawyer," he said, managing to jerk her from the entranced haze she was in danger of slipping into. "He's been offered a prestigious contract in Europe that will run for at least the next five years."

Since he'd left the coffee shop that afternoon, Bobbie had mentally run through at least a dozen scenarios about what Gabe wanted to discuss. His ex-wife's husband had *not* been one of them. "Um…congratulations to him?"

Gabe's lips twisted. "I know. This makes no sense to you. What has Fiona told you about me?"

"Besides you being successful and very, *very* eligible?" His hooded blue gaze sharpened on her face and she managed a wry smile that hopefully hid the shivers dancing down her spine. "We're usually busy talking about what's going on at Golden Ability. It doesn't seem to leave a lot of time to chatter about her family. Or mine." She reasoned that the white lie was better than admitting how much his grandmother praised his qualities.

His dark head tipped a few centimeters. "My wife and I divorced nearly eight years ago." He slowly turned the wine glass on top of the white linen table covering. "It wasn't what you'd call amicable."

"I'm sorry."

"I share plenty of the responsibility in that," he admitted.

"But that's beside the point. What is the point, are my kids. Steph was awarded custody of them when we split. The ink was barely dry on our divorce decree when she became Mrs. Ethan Walker, and then within a year they'd moved to Switzerland. It had been hard enough to keep her to the terms of my visitation before she moved, but after—" He shook his head. "A few years ago, though, her husband's job brought them back here to Seattle. Supposedly to stay, so I decided to move here, too. It was the only sure way I had of reminding my kids that I was their father—not just some guy who came to visit for a few days once a year."

Bobbie's heart squeezed at the pain on his face.

"Anyway, my business partner remained in Colorado, and I started up another branch here. We're making it when a lot of companies aren't, but it hasn't been easy."

The shivers that had been dancing down Bobbie's spine suddenly felt like jagged little spears instead, as realization dawned. "Harrison Hunt might be a family friend, but I have no influence when it comes to HuntCom."

Gabe's brows yanked together. "What are you talking about?"

She sat up straighter in her chair. "It's not like I don't understand. Or…or sympathize. Even in this economy, HuntCom still has building projects going on all over the world." If they weren't building a new manufacturing facility for themselves, they were building something else. She knew, because she had to make an appearance at least once a year at the board of directors' meeting, at which time she always gave her proxy to Gray, who'd been running the privately-held company since Harry's health had forced him into retirement. "But the best I can do is get you a name." She'd have to call Harry and find out who the chief architect was now. Since J.T.—one of Gray's younger brothers—had vacated the position to hang out his own shingle in Portland, she couldn't even hazard a guess who was responsible for the property development arm of the enormous company.

"I'm not looking to do business with HuntCom," Gabe said slowly. "Is that what you expected?"

"It's what most people expect once they realize I have a connection there." Her chin lifted. "You're hardly the first." Lawrence had simply been the most recent.

Gabe was silent for a moment, his gaze measuring. "As it happens," he finally said evenly, "I don't give a flip about HuntCom. The only thing I'm trying to do is keep my ex-wife from moving my kids to another damn country again."

She blinked.

He shoved to his feet and paced along the narrow aisle between the empty tables. "If the judge doesn't approve my petition for joint custody, there's not one thing I'll be able to do to stop her." He grimaced. "Short of kidnapping them."

Bobbie reached for the wineglass he'd abandoned and took a long drink.

"I'm kidding." His voice was dark. "The last thing I need is more trouble with the law."

More trouble?

She took another sip of wine and then carefully set the glass down. "I'm sorry about your children, but what does that have to do with me?"

"I need a wife."

Her hand twitched violently. She knocked the glass right over, sending deep-red liquid pouring across the perfect white linen tablecloth. She hastily flipped up the side of the cloth to keep it from running onto the floor. "I beg your pardon?"

"Not a real wife." He shoved one hand through his hair. "The last thing I want is to get married again. Once was enough to last a lifetime." He visibly shuddered. "But I need to make the impression that I'll have a wife, soon. Ray—my attorney—wants me to have a real one, of course, though he swears he'll deny it if the truth ever gets out."

"I'm not even sure what the truth *is*." She watched him cautiously. "You want me to pretend to be married to you?"

"I want everyone to think we're *getting* married." He pulled the chair out from behind the table to straddle it directly in front of her. "It won't have to be for long. My custody hearing is scheduled for right after Thanksgiving. As long as the judge believes that I can provide Todd and Lissi with what Steph and Ethan provide—a stable family life—there's no reason why he would deny my petition for joint custody."

"And that's going to prevent your ex-wife from moving again to Europe?"

He grimaced. "Nothing prevents Steph from doing what she wants. But she won't be able to keep the kids with her for the entire time. Instead of the sixteen hours a week I'm allowed now—assuming it doesn't inconvenience her—she'll have to agree to new terms. *Joint* terms. Ray says that there's a possibility that I could have them for the entire school year, even. That they'd only go to Europe for vacation and holiday breaks." He grabbed her hands. "The only good thing to come out of my marriage were Lisette and Todd. And for too long, they barely even knew I was their father. I'm not going to lose them again."

"But we'd be lying. You have no intention of marrying me."

"Being married shouldn't matter. Technically, it's not even supposed to," Gabe said. "I should have been awarded joint custody in the first place."

"Why weren't you?"

"Because I made the mistake of loving my wife." His voice went flat. "And when I caught her in bed—*our* bed—with Ethan, I lost my temper." His hands curled. "I decked him and got charged with assault as a result. Then I stupidly followed that up by crawling into a whiskey bottle for a while. The assault charge was dropped eventually, but the damage was done. The bastard ended up with my wife *and* my kids." His lips twisted. "Proof that the lawyers in his family are better than the lawyers in mine."

She let out a long breath. "No wonder you wanted some privacy to talk." Buying time—and not exactly sure why— she gathered up the wet tablecloth and took it into the back, where she ran water and left it to soak. Then she returned to the front, where she found him pacing between the tables. But he stopped when he spotted her.

She had to remind herself that the intensity in his gaze had everything to do with his children and nothing to do with her personally. But she still had to concentrate on keeping her knees steady, though she pressed her back against the hard edge of the wine bar for extra support. "I can understand your position," she began carefully, "but I don't think I'm the right person for the job."

"Why? You have some secret scandal in your past that's worse than me being charged with assault?"

"No. No scandals." Humiliation wasn't scandal, was it? She tugged nervously at the silky red scarf that was holding her hair back in a low ponytail. "It's just, well, I like you."

He waited. "So?"

She should have just made up a scandal. It would have been simpler. And much less mortifying. "I mean, I—" she swallowed, feeling foolish. "I *like* you."

"Ah." Add a faint curve of his mobile lips to that laser-like gaze and she felt even more out of her depth. "Why would that be a problem?"

She grimaced. "Do I have to spell it out?"

"Apparently."

"It's one-sided," she said baldly. "And nobody would believe you could be seriously engaged to me, anyway."

He eyed her. "Because I'm old enough to be your father?"

She let out a half laugh. "You're forty-one. Hardly old enough to be my father." And the feelings he roused in her weren't the least bit daughterly.

"How'd you know how old I was?"

"Fiona," she admitted, realizing she'd given herself away much too easily.

"Thought you didn't talk about your families much."

Her face was getting hot. "All right. I asked. Is that a crime?"

"Not at all. And you're twenty-seven." That little smile was back. "I asked."

She didn't know what to say to that, so for once in her life, she kept her mouth shut.

He walked up to her, not stopping until the toes of his shoes were practically bumping hers. He rested his hands on the wine bar to either side of her.

She swallowed, more aware than ever just how alone they were. And just how tall he was. And how broad his shoulders were. And…how incredible he smelled.

"For the record—" his head dropped and his whisper tickled at her ear, not helping her case one whit "—it's not one-sided. I *like* you, too. Maybe you didn't notice that when you were telling me to make it look good. It's one of the reasons why I think a sudden engagement between us would be… convincing." He shifted slightly until he was looking her right in the eyes. "So let's get that cleared up right now." He closed his mouth over hers.

The taste of him went straight to her head. Her joints went soft. And instead of pushing against him, her palms slowly slid up his chest, over his shoulders. Colors splashed in her mind and her head fell back when the low sound he made filled her mouth as his kiss deepened. Lengthened.

And then he was tearing away, pulling in a whistling breath.

She was shaking. She realized his hand was in her hair, cradling her neck. Beyond that, she couldn't seem to gather a functioning thought.

"Think about it." His voice was a low caress, stirring a curl of hair at her temple. "I'll give you whatever you want in return."

Her addled brain might as well have been an old engine, coughing and stuttering, before it finally fired and she began to understand what he was saying. He meant think about pretending to be his fiancée. Her bones felt liquefied and her muscles felt shaky, but she still managed to shake her head. "I don't want anything. It's not a good idea. One-sided or two-sided. It's still not a good idea." She couldn't stand to find herself, once again, a hindrance to someone she cared about. "You should find someone else."

"There is no one else."

"Someone you've dated—"

"I don't date." He grimaced. "Not anymore. Look. Just give yourself a day or two to think about it," he advised. "Think about Fiona. As young at heart as she is, she is not a young woman. How many chances will she have to enjoy her only great-grandchildren if they're out of the country again for the better part of what's left of their childhood?"

He couldn't have found a more vulnerable button to push. Fiona was extremely dear to Bobbie.

"All right," she agreed reluctantly. "I'll *think* about it. But you—" she lifted her finger and jabbed it into the center of his hard chest "—would be wise to spend the next day or two thinking of someone more suitable to make your pretend fiancée."

"Believe me, Bobbie. You're very suitable."

She managed a smile, but there was no humor in it. "You'll change your mind," she promised.

People always did.

Chapter Four

By Saturday afternoon, Bobbie felt certain that Gabe had done just what she'd expected. Changed his mind.

He hadn't shown up that morning to finish the grout work on her newly tiled bathroom floor. Nor had he called to explain his absence. His silence didn't seem to fit with the man she thought she was coming to know, but it definitely served as a reminder that just because he was Fiona's grandson, didn't mean that she really knew him at all.

So they'd shared a few kisses and a few confidences. What did that mean in the scheme of things? She'd shared a lot more than that with her ex-fiancé, thinking they would be spending a lifetime together.

Only now, Lawrence had a sleekly elegant blond woman with a stellar pedigree wearing his wedding ring on her finger. She'd been the one standing next to him at the podium after his re-election, smiling her perfectly aligned smile, waving her perfectly manicured hands and charming the press with her perfectly timed, perfectly worded comments. She'd been the one he'd loved all along, even when he'd been sweeping Bobbie off her feet.

"Ah, Bobbie, dear." Fiona's voice interrupted the gathering steam of her memories. "Ujjayi breathing is meant to be relaxing and energizing. Aim for the soothing sound of an ocean. Not the menacing sound of a freight train heading for derailment."

Bobbie opened her eyes and looked across at Fiona's wry expression.

They were sitting cross-legged on yoga mats on the floor in the middle of Fiona's spacious sunroom. The lengthening sunlight gilded the plants surrounding the room and water dripped soothingly over the small rock fountain in the midst of them. It was a perfect place to practice yoga, and they'd done so at least once a week for months—well before Bobbie had moved into the carriage house.

"Sorry." She rolled her head around her shoulders and drew in a long breath. Usually, practicing yoga was one of the few times that she could count on to get out of her own head. To let go of whatever nonsense plagued her thoughts during the day, to thoroughly de-stress.

Why hadn't Gabe at least called?

"You know," Fiona said, unwinding her legs and pushing to her bare feet, "there are times that call for yoga, and there are times that call for cocktails." She grinned. "I'm thinking... cocktail."

Bobbie laughed and straightened her legs. "A true yogi wouldn't even consider consuming alcohol."

"Fortunately, I have no aspirations in that direction," Fiona assured dryly. "And what does that song say? It's five o'clock somewhere?" She gestured. "Come with me."

Bobbie pushed to her feet and followed her friend out of the sunroom. She tightened the band holding her hair on the top of her head and tried not to look out the windows for some sign of Gabe's truck as they walked through the house. When she did sneak a peek, all she saw was the gardening crew working on the lush landscape and the catering truck, there to set up the outdoor tent that would house the dance floor for the party tomorrow night that Fiona didn't even want.

When they reached Fiona's office, which overlooked the half-acre sweep of lawn leading to the carriage house, Fiona waved at the massive leather wing chairs angled in front of the fireplace. "Sit." She moved to the ornate cabinet standing against the wall.

Bobbie sat, watching her elderly friend pull open the cabinet to reveal an extremely well-stocked bar. Fiona had once told her that she hadn't changed a single thing in the office after her husband had died. It was the only room she had left untouched in the entire house, because it felt like he was still with her whenever she worked in there.

"I meant to thank you again for helping out at the office yesterday. It took months to get an appointment with the community affairs rep from Cragmin, and I'd have hated to reschedule."

Bobbie shrugged, though she still was a little surprised that Fiona had managed to double-book her schedule the way she had. She'd been across town making another funding request when the manufacturing company's community affairs manager had shown up at Golden's office and Fiona had called Bobbie in a rush to fill in for her. "I'm always willing. You know that, though I'm a poor substitute for you."

Fiona waved the cocktail shaker as she pulled it off the shelf. "You did wonderfully well, as I knew you would. I got an email last night from the CEO that we were on the short list for the grant." She added ice from a small, cleverly hidden freezer to the shaker. "But enough of that. How are your mother and sisters?"

"All fine. I've been helping Tommi at the bistro this past week. One of her servers has been on vacation."

Fiona was nodding as she added a shot of this and a dash of that. "I wish my daughter-in-law would have thought to ask your sister to cater this thing tomorrow." She capped the shaker and shook it so vigorously that Bobbie wondered if she was mentally wringing Astrid Gannon's neck. "Then at least the food would have been wonderful."

"I'm sure the food will be fine," Bobbie soothed. "And I think Tommi has enough on her plate with the bistro being as busy as it is." She'd thought her sister had seemed particularly stressed the past week, but of course, Tommi had simply dismissed the very idea when Bobbie had tried to broach the subject. And since Bobbie hadn't wanted to answer Tommi's questions about Gabe's presence at the bistro the other night either, she'd kept most of her thoughts to herself. "You've said before that your daughter-in-law hosts some magnificent parties."

"Trust you to remember that," Fiona muttered darkly. She poured the pale yellow contents of the shaker into two martini glasses and handed one to Bobbie. "Cheers."

Bobbie lifted her glass in salute and sipped gingerly, well used to Fiona's less-than-delicate hand when it came to mixing a cocktail. Predictably, the drink was light on lemon and heavy on vodka. "I think it's nice that your family wants to celebrate your birthday with you."

Fiona waved her hand. "It would be nice if it were just family and a few friends." She sank down into a corner of the opposite chair. "Instead, I believe Astrid has invited half of the world. She never even asked who I would like to invite. I suppose she was afraid I'd invite someone *unsuitable*." She made a face. "Like my own employees and volunteers."

"Well, it'll be over soon enough."

"I'm not sure I appreciate a phrase like that at my age," Fiona replied dryly.

Bobbie couldn't help but laugh, even though she was immediately reminded of Gabe's words about his grandmother. "You're one of the youngest people I know. And it has nothing to do with the calendar."

Fiona leaned forward and patted Bobbie's knee. "You're a dear. Now tell me what you think of Gabriel."

Bobbie nearly choked on her cocktail. She swallowed, trying not to gasp a little at the strong alcohol. "He's very... handy." She lifted her shoulder and hoped Fiona would blame the color in her cheeks on the drink. "The work he's doing around the carriage house has been great."

Fiona's eyes sparkled. "Yes. But what do you think of *him?*"

For a moment, Bobbie wondered if Gabe had told his grandmother about their unconventional meeting. Or about what had happened since.

But then she dismissed it as unlikely.

"I think he's—" *sexy, handsome, unreasonably attractive* "—nice," she managed weakly. "He certainly loves his children."

Fiona nodded. Her eyes narrowed slightly as she sipped her cocktail. "He'd do anything for them."

"Mmm." Bobbie took another too-hasty drink that burned all the way down her throat. Already her head was beginning to swim a little and she quickly set the glass on the small table next to the chair while she could still set it safely without spilling it. "I imagine they'll all be here for your party tomorrow evening?"

"I'd certainly prefer Todd and Lisette over their mother's presence, but Astrid hasn't included the children."

Bobbie blinked. "Gabe's...ex-wife is coming?" Given

their strained relationship, she hadn't expected that. Had he exaggerated the situation?

"Yes. I know it sounds odd. But Astrid and Stephanie's mother are dear friends and for some reason, Astrid still believes that Stephanie and Gabe will reconcile. Doesn't seem to matter that Stephanie betrayed Gabe in the worst possible way, or that she's doing her level best to keep Gabe's children from him as much as she can. She picked Stephanie for Gabe years ago, and can't bring herself to realize that her choice stunk." Fiona let out an exasperated sigh. "The woman doesn't even know her own son. And *my* son doesn't seem any better. Even though I myself haven't seen Stephanie in years, I'm not holding out hope that she'd have the good taste to decline the invitation." Fiona drained her glass and with no seeming regard for the fine crystal, set it on the side table with a clunk. "I think *you* should come to the party. I don't know why I didn't think of it before."

Bobbie straightened her spine. "What?"

Fiona lifted her eyebrows. "It's *my* birthday party. I should be able to invite at least one person that I want to be there, shouldn't I?"

"Well, of course, but—"

"Then it's done." She pushed to her feet. "Sadly, it's black tie." She rolled her eyes. "Astrid's doing, of course. You have something suitable? Maybe a dress left over from that drip of a fiancé you had?"

"I have a gown or two." Shoved in the back of her closet because she didn't have the good sense to get rid of clothing that she never wore—or never planned to wear again. Until her involvement with Lawrence, the only times she'd had to dress formally were for the annual Christmas parties that her Uncle Harry always threw. "But honestly, Fiona, I'll feel like I'm gatecrashing." She knew Astrid Gannon had sent out the engraved invitations weeks ago, because Fiona had been bemoaning the upcoming party ever since.

"Frankly, I feel like *I* am gatecrashing," Fiona countered. "Mark my words. It will be stuffy and boring. But I beg you. Just come for a few minutes. Long enough to give me *someone* besides Gabriel I can honestly say how nice it is to see."

"One of these days I'm going to learn how to say no to you, and mean it." Bobbie stood up also. Her head felt light from just those few sips of her cocktail. She needed to eat.

Fiona smiled victoriously and tucked her arm through Bobbie's as they strolled through the house toward the kitchen. "You'll be the belle of the ball."

"Now I *know* your cocktail has gone to your head," Bobbie accused wryly. "Since you know as well as I do how unlikely that will be. If you want a belle, you'd need Frankie or Georgie." Both of her older sisters could sweep into any setting and have the masses charmed with barely a flick of their fingers. It was a talent they'd come by naturally from their mother. Even Tommi possessed it—when she could be dragged out from the kitchen, where she usually ended up even when she wasn't the chef.

"Give yourself a little more credit." Fiona pulled open the back door for Bobbie. "You might surprise yourself."

"I doubt it." Bobbie hugged Fiona. "But I'll be there, for you."

"Be where?"

Bobbie straightened like a shot, spinning around so fast that she nearly tipped over.

Gabe's hand shot out, catching her shoulder. "Steady there."

She didn't know which was worse. The dizzying effect of Fiona's lethal cocktail, the sudden thrill of Gabe's touch, or the fact that both were probably as plain as the nose on her face to Fiona, Gabe *and* his daughter and son, who were standing on the porch beside him.

"At the party tomorrow," Fiona answered, which was good because Bobbie didn't seem able to make her mouth work in concert with her brain. "Bobbie's coming, too. Isn't that lovely?"

"Sure." Gabe's gaze rested on her face and she couldn't tell what he was thinking to save her life.

What she was thinking about was what he'd asked her to do. And that she knew she should refuse. Again. Which wasn't something that she could very well tell him right then and there. Not with his grandmother and kids witnessing her non-conversation with him. "I, um, I need to get home," she finally managed to say to the air in general. She glanced at Fiona. "See you tomorrow." She moved past Gabe without looking at him directly, and managed to smile at his kids as she quickly ran down the porch steps.

"I'll come with you." His deep voice followed her, putting an abrupt end to her hasty departure. "Still need to finish that tile job."

She looked back, not meeting his eyes or Fiona's, and nodded jerkily. "Okay."

"Lissi, Todd, you go inside with Grandma and finish your homework."

Bobbie realized belatedly that both of his children were sporting extremely fat, heavy-looking backpacks.

"We'll go out for dinner when I've finished at Ms. Fairchild's," he added.

They both nodded without argument and went inside the main house with Fiona.

"Ready?" Gabe prompted when Bobbie didn't start moving again toward the carriage house.

She stopped staring after the children and started walking instead. Even without letting her gaze sidle toward him, she was excruciatingly aware of him. "Your kids seemed rather subdued."

"I guess that's one way of putting it."

She couldn't help herself. She looked right at him, taking in his unshaven jaw and bloodshot eyes. "And you look like you haven't slept in days. What's wrong?"

"Nothing that another ten hours in every day wouldn't cure." He took her elbow, helping her along the uneven stone pathway that led to her door, even though he had to know that she'd walked over it hundreds of times before. "One of my construction managers had a car accident a few days ago and I've had to fill in on the job site for him." They stopped at the door of the cottage and he waited for her to unlock it.

"Is he going to be all right?"

He gave her an odd look. "Yeah. Broke a few bones, but he'll probably be nagging me to get him back at the site before the doctor even says it's okay." He followed her inside. "You're the only one who has asked that."

Her little carriage house felt cozy at the best of times. With him standing in the center of her living room between the leather chair that she'd purloined from her mother's basement and the outdated floral-patterned but immensely comfortable couch she'd bought at a consignment store, the space felt even smaller. More intimate. "I'm sorry? I'm sure his coworkers wanted to know how—"

He waved his hand. "Yeah. Of course folks on the crew and at the office asked." He ran his hand tiredly down his face, then around to the back of his neck. "Don't mind me." He turned toward the short, narrow hall that would lead him to the bathroom, only to do an about-face a second later.

She nearly bumped into him and he caught her shoulders in his hands again. "Sorry." He stepped around her. "Tools are in my truck."

She chewed the inside of her lip, watching him leave.

He hadn't brought up the business about her posing as his fiancée. Maybe he wouldn't. Maybe he'd changed his mind so thoroughly that he didn't even want to bring it up.

As if she'd have forgotten it if he didn't.

She exhaled roughly and headed into the kitchen to let the dogs out of their kennels. The light on her answering machine was blinking, and she poked the button before opening the cage.

"Bobbie, this is Quentin Rich."

She glanced at the machine as she snapped on Archimedes's leash. "Who?"

"We met at the Hunt Christmas party last year. I heard you were available and I thought it would be nice to get together again. Maybe dinner? Call me." The caller reeled off his number.

Bobbie looked down at Archimedes. "Do you remember him?"

The dog's tongue lolled out of his mouth. He gave her a goofy look.

"Me either. And that party was ten months ago." She erased the message and called Zeus, who'd been patiently waiting. With their leashes on, they both bolted out the front door, pulling her along with them. They veered away from their original target—the bushes—when they spotted Gabe and raced toward him instead.

A grin stretched across his face, erasing years of tiredness, as he set down his bucket filled with tiling tools and crouched down to greet them. "How you doing, Zeus?" He rubbed one dog down, then the other. "Archie? You staying away from eating Bobbie's couch cushions?"

"I'm surprised." Bobbie slowly walked closer, giving the leashes more play. "Not even Fiona can tell them apart."

Gabe figured it was safer all around for him to focus on

the oversized puppies slathering slobber over his hands and arms than on Bobbie.

Or he'd be the one likely to start slobbering over himself.

He was used to being around beautiful women. Hell, he'd been married to one, even if she'd turned out to be carved from ice. So what was it about *this* woman that turned his guts inside out? He knew he should look at her and think "too young," but her age was truthfully the last thing he had on his mind when she was around.

Maybe that explained midlife crises…

"They've got their differences," he pointed out a little doggedly. "Archie here has a quirk in the way he holds his ears. And Zeus just looks at you like he wants to lie on your feet and sleep for a week. Which is a thought I've had myself lately."

Bobbie laughed softly, and he couldn't help himself. He looked up at her.

She wore stretchy black pants that clung to every inch of her shapely legs from knee to hip. And even though she had some gauzy white shirt on, it didn't do diddly to disguise the lush curves adoringly displayed by a sleeveless black top beneath it that ended well above her waist. What the thin fabric did succeed at was taunting him mercilessly with the filmy silhouette of those inches of bare skin exposed between the top and the pants. Bare skin that nipped in over a tiny waist that made everything else seem even more…curved.

He stifled on oath, dragging his gaze away.

Archimedes slapped his gold, feathered tail on the ground, still grinning sloppily as if he read Gabe's mind all too easily.

And maybe the dogs did, because Zeus trotted back over to his mistress, leaning his healthy, growing body protectively against Bobbie's legs. Her hand dropped to her side, her slender fingers sliding over his well-shaped head. The dog looked as if he wanted to purr. "They're both good boys," she said. "Once they go to their trainer, I'm sure they'll end up being excellent assistance dogs."

Gabe distracted Archimedes from sniffing the bag of grout sitting inside the bucket. "How many puppies have you raised for Fiona's group?"

"Counting these two?" She didn't hesitate. "Seventeen."

"That's a lot of dogs. You have them for nearly two years, don't you?"

"They usually go into training around eighteen months. I generally get them when they're about eight weeks old, but sometimes it's later because they've been moved from another raiser for some reason. These guys were littermates, so I got them at the same time. Usually, I have a mixture of ages. One time I had four dogs at once." She grinned wryly. "Needless to say, my mother and sisters thought I'd lost a few screws. And it was a little…crazy. Compared to that, just having these two now is pretty quiet, actually. I have photo albums of all of my puppies on the shelf in the hall."

The shelf he'd nearly knocked over the day he'd brought the tile in for her bathroom floor. "But in the end, you give them all up."

She looked down at the dog beside her. "That's the point. I'm just the puppy raiser. Not one of Fiona's dog trainers."

"Why not?"

"Because this is something I'm actually good at. All of the puppies I've raised have been successfully partnered with someone. Guide dogs for the blind, a few hearing dogs, a few service dogs. One even became a search and rescue dog out in Montana." She lifted her shoulder and the filmy shirt shimmied around her hips. "It's my one part in helping someone else's life be a little easier." Her cheeks colored and her eyes looked like fog clouding Rainier. "I know that probably sounds—"

"—like Fiona talking."

She shook her head, her lips curving slightly. "That wasn't what I was going to say."

"But it's the truth." For several generations, the Gannon family had had nearly every advantage in life. But instead of simply donating her money to some cause she believed in, his grandmother had spent most of Gabe's life personally involved in one. She'd founded her small agency that trained and placed assistance dogs around the country, and even though the rest of Gabe's family thought she was more than a little eccentric for working so hard for so long when she didn't have to, he'd admired her for it.

In her way, Fiona Gannon was as much the oddball in the family as he was.

"You're doing a good thing," he told Bobbie now. Truthfully. He pushed tiredly to his feet. "And for the record, I'm certain that you're good at a lot more than raising puppies. But I still think it's gotta be damn hard to give them up when it's time."

Her lashes swept down for a moment. "It's always hard to say goodbye. But I get to meet the person they're partnered with when they finish their training, and the dogs always remember me." She looked up then with a crooked grin. "And I receive a ton of Christmas cards with the dogs' pictures in them."

"Well, you're still a better person than I am." He picked up the heavy bucket, lifting it away from Archimedes's inquisitive snout. "I probably wouldn't want to let them go."

"You really don't have to finish the floor today, you know. It's not going anywhere. Take a break."

Her gaze danced over him, then away again, and he wished to hell he knew what he could do to ease her obvious nervousness. But he wasn't ready to hear her tell him again that he was on his own when it came to the fake fiancée business, so they were both stuck. Unfortunately, every day that ticked past was a day that took him closer to the judge's courtroom.

"It's not like you haven't been working hard enough already, covering for your injured guy," she continued.

Unlike his ex-wife, who'd quite vocally considered Gabe's injured worker to be a personal inconvenience to her. "It won't take me long to grout the floor." Not when her bathroom was barely large enough to turn around in.

"And then you'll go and have dinner with your children?"

"I'll take them to dinner," he clarified. "They're none too happy right now to begin with, since their mother decided to go to D.C. with Ethan a few days ago for some meetings. The last thing to help that situation would be my cooking."

She worried her soft lower lip with the pearly edge of her teeth for a moment. "Lisette and Todd have been staying with you, then? When is their mother coming back?"

"Tomorrow, and it was surprising that Steph was willing to leave them with me." Particularly when she'd learned he was putting in even more hours on the job than usual, until she'd realized the advantage the situation might afford her. "But then she realized that I might do such a rotten job of caring for them full-time for a few days that she'll have extra ammunition against me when we go to court again."

Bobbie's soft lips tightened. "No wonder you're tired. Extra work on that job site on top of your usual load, plus having the kids and getting them to and from school?" Shaking her head, she walked over to him and wrapped her free hand around the bucket handle, unsuccessfully trying to dislodge his hand in the process. "Give me that. My floor can definitely wait."

The curls coiled on top of her head tickled his chin, smelling faintly of lemon.

He still didn't let go of the bucket. "I'll let the floor wait if you'll come to dinner with me and the kids."

He had to steel his nerves against the soft gaze she turned toward him. "I think that's bribery or something."

Bribery and a good dose of self-torture. "Is it working?"

"You're as bad as your grandmother," she accused. But there was a faint smile on her soft, soft lips.

"That's probably one of the nicer things I've been accused of," he admitted wryly. "Is that a yes?"

"Yes. To dinner," she added quickly.

But he didn't mind the qualification.

After a little time with his kids, maybe she'd see that one more "yes" would be just another way of making someone else's life a little easier for a while.

Namely, his.

And if she did, the trick then would be for all of them to get through it unscathed when their arrangement was no longer necessary.

Chapter Five

The next evening, Bobbie tilted her head sideways and studied her reflection in the full-length mirror attached to the front of her closet door. The hem of the pewter-colored gown was pooling on the carpet around her bare feet, but that would be solved well enough when she put on her high heels. Squinting at herself, she gathered up two fists of ringlets and piled her hair on top of her head.

"I don't know, Zeus. What do you think? Does it look like I'm trying to play dress-up? What do you think Gabe will think?" She looked at the dog's reflection in the mirror. He was watching her with patient eyes from where he lay on the floor at the foot of her bed that was strewn with a half-dozen gowns, already tried and rejected.

The only gown left was the one she was wearing. She'd bought it on a shopping spree with Frankie—with her fashionable sister's mild approval—shortly before Lawrence had dumped her. She'd never actually worn it out. She would have returned it to the store, in fact, except it had been a clearance dress and it had been less embarrassing just to shove it in the back of her closet than go back to the store and admit she hadn't needed the dress after all.

Not when her fiancé had decided *she* didn't need to accompany him to any more fund-raisers. Or to anything else, for that matter. He particularly didn't want her working on his reelection campaign. What was the point, since she didn't have a pipeline into the treasures of the HuntCom empire after all?

She let go of her hair and it fell down past her shoulders, settling into its usual disarray. Her hand swept down the folds of gleaming fabric that fell in a column from the empire waist. The gown had tiny cap sleeves that were little more than wide straps hugging the points of her shoulders. The front of the bodice was cut low and straight across her breasts, leaving more of her cleavage on view than Bobbie was accustomed to. But Frankie hadn't vetoed the dress, so Bobbie could only cross her fingers in the hope that it suited her as much as anything could.

Her phone jangled, startling her from her critical study of herself, and she picked up the extension on the nightstand. "Hello?"

"Bobbie?" The deep voice was unfamiliar. "This is Quentin. Quentin Rich. I've been hoping to reach you."

She wrinkled her nose. The guy who'd left the phone message. Tucking the phone against her shoulder, she stepped over Archimedes, who was sleeping in the doorway, and went into the bathroom to rummage through the drawer for some hairpins. Where were the sparkly ones that Georgie had given her for Christmas? "Right. Quentin." Whom she still couldn't remember. "How are you?"

"Great. Just great. Listen, I was wondering if you'd like to meet up again. There's a new restaurant that's been getting rave reviews I've been dying to take you to."

She lifted her eyebrows, a little taken aback by his enthusiasm. "Really. Dying, huh?"

"I know you'd love the place," he continued confidently. "You actually dine in the dark. So you don't even see what's on your plate. It's all very...tactile."

"Messy, you mean." She couldn't help but laugh, as it finally came to her when they'd met. "Which seemed fitting, since you saw me spill a plate of hors d'oeuvres on myself at last year's Christmas party."

"It was hardly your fault," he assured quickly. "And that wasn't it at all."

She rolled her eyes and slammed the drawer shut. Maybe the hair clips were in her jewelry box. "As I recall, you were pitching some sort of software to HuntCom. How'd that go?" She hitched up her dress again, stepping over the dogs on her way to her dresser.

"Great. Just great. Mr. Hunt's taken quite a personal interest lately, too."

A stray thought had her hesitating. "Which Mr. Hunt?" As far as she knew, Gray was way too occupied with helming the worldwide company while keeping up with his wife and their kids to get personally involved with a software project that even she remembered had been relatively small and unexciting.

"Harrison," Quentin provided smoothly. "I'll admit it's pretty flattering to have such a pioneer taking an interest in my work—"

The man prattled on, but Bobbie barely heard.

Harry.

First it had been Tim Boering. And now it was this guy. She hadn't had so much as a date since Lawrence dumped her, but now, in a matter of weeks, she'd had two men claiming interest. And both were connected to Harry?

Suspicion niggled at her, but she dismissed it. Admittedly, Harry was one of the most manipulative—if oddly charming—men that Bobbie knew. But he knew what a blow the whole Lawrence episode had been; she couldn't imagine why he'd nudge guys her way now. He never had before.

If anything, he was probably looking for some innocuous person to keep Quentin and his latest software project safely entertained.

Satisfied with her reasoning, she snatched up the sparkling hair clips shaped like daisies where they were buried beneath a jumble of inexpensive earrings and necklaces that would have given the orderly Georgie fits. "Listen, Quentin, I'm sorry, but I'm just on my way out." Nearly.

"Ah. Then why don't I call you tomorrow?"

"No!" She winced a little at her own vehemence. "I mean, I appreciate you thinking of me, but I'm—"

"—seeing someone again already, I suppose."

She opened her mouth to deny it, but the words didn't come. A vision of Gabe and his children crowding around her coffee table the night before to wolf down the best pizza Seattle had to offer swam inside her head much too readily.

"Well…" She forced a little laugh, hoping he'd draw his own conclusions without her actually having to tell an outright lie. She'd never claimed that she wasn't a coward. And she didn't want to hurt his feelings any more than she'd wanted to hurt Boering's. They were associates of her Uncle Harry's, after all.

"Message understood," Quentin was saying. "But seriously, if you change your mind, you have my number."

"Right." Actually, she didn't, since she'd erased his earlier message with no thought or regret whatsoever. "I'll keep that in mind. I've really got to run now."

"Sure. Good night, Bobbie."

"'Bye, Quentin." She quickly disconnected and tossed the phone on her jumbled bed. "Zeus, remind me to tell Uncle Harry I'm not the welcoming committee lady the next time I see him, will you?"

Zeus yawned hugely, then lowered his head down onto his outstretched paws.

"Thanks for the support," Bobbie muttered. She stepped over him again to reach the mirror and pinned back several curls of hair with Georgie's fancy little clips. Then she pushed her feet into the shimmery silver shoes with the deadly spiked heels that Frankie had insisted were made to go with the gown and grabbed the long, black cashmere coat that had been a birthday present from her mother two years earlier.

There was no need for her purse since she was just going across to the main house. She swung the coat around her shoulders and snatched up the box containing the scrapbook she'd made as a gift for Fiona, then headed outside.

The enormous tent that had been erected on the graceful lawn was surrounded by little white lights that sparkled wetly in the damp night air. She could hear the band playing some old, sedate melody that sounded more in keeping with a museum opening than a birthday celebration and as she neared the tent, she could see that only a few couples were moving about on the dance floor. The floor was surrounded by linen and crystal-covered round tables, most of them occupied, and the nervousness that Bobbie had been more or less successfully holding at bay since she'd woken up that morning came barreling down the chute.

A uniformed young man carrying a gilded tray of filled champagne flutes crossed her path. "Wait." The heels of her fancy shoes sunk into the grass a little as she took a step after him. "Can I—"

"Certainly." He waited for her to take one of the flutes, which she did carefully lest she knock the other glasses over.

"Thanks." She took a quick drink as her gaze skimmed over the crowd. "You wouldn't happen to know where the birthday girl is, would you?"

"Inside, I believe." The young man continued on his way toward the guests.

Bobbie looked up at the deep terrace that led into the house. There were tables and guests there, too. She took another sip of champagne, chiding herself inwardly for feeling so nervous.

She'd spent several thoroughly enjoyable hours with Gabe and his children the evening before and he hadn't uttered one single syllable about his suggestion that she pretend to be his fiancée for the benefit of his child custody case. If anything, he'd treated her more like a sister. Certainly not like someone he'd twisted inside out with his very kiss.

And it wasn't as if he hadn't had an opportunity to talk to her privately, because after they'd ravenously consumed the pizza that she'd talked him into letting her order while he'd been wedged into her bathroom working on the floor, Todd and Lisette had been totally occupied playing with the dogs in the yard outside.

For all she knew, he'd come to his senses and realized the potholes in his thinking, so there would be no need for her to get into all the reasons why going along with his scheme was a bad idea.

Tightening her arm around the large gift-wrapped box, she went up the shallow steps to the terrace. On the way, she recognized Kanya, the community affairs manager from the company that Fiona was hoping to get that substantial grant from, and stopped long enough to exchange pleasantries. Hers was the only familiar face that Bobbie saw.

But when she spotted Gabe standing just inside the open

French doors of the living room, she forgot how to speak altogether.

Over the years, Bobbie figured she'd seen countless men in countless tuxedos. But not once had she ever been dumbstruck by the very sight. He looked...magnificent.

It wasn't just the formal wear, though the midnight-blue jacket and trousers were miles away from his usual jeans and T-shirt. He'd slicked back his dark hair from his face and when he shifted, looking out over the terrace, even from several yards away she was struck by the sharp angles of his handsome face, by the startling clarity of his blue, blue eyes.

And then those eyes turned her way.

His lips turned up at the corners and even though she knew it was fanciful of her, when his hand left his pocket to lift in her direction, it all seemed to happen in an achingly slow motion, accompanied by a swell of music from the band.

Her stomach dipped and swayed woozily, and she had the ridiculous sense that her life, in that moment, had just changed forever.

"So we're hoping to get an answer for Fiona on the grant," she heard Kanya saying, though it might as well have been gibberish.

Bobbie dragged in a shaking breath and swallowed hard, mumbling something—hopefully coherent—to Kanya before she headed toward Gabe and his extended palm.

Only when she neared the open doors did she notice the other people he was with. Two men easily as tall as he was, though not quite as broad in the shoulders, but with hair equally as dark as Gabe's. She guessed that they were his older brothers, Liam and Paul. And the women with them were undoubtedly their wives—who looked like cookie-cutter socialites with their upswept hair, diamonds circling their long throats and strapless black gowns showing their svelte figures to their best advantage.

They were so picture-perfect that Bobbie felt even more like a schoolgirl playing at dress-up.

Then Gabe stepped out onto the terrace, closing the distance between them. "I was beginning to think I was going to have to come and find you," he greeted. His gaze ran over her. "But the wait was worth every second. Let me take that." He plucked the box out from beneath her arm. "Heavy," he commented.

She was still shaking, and she ordered herself to get a grip. "I made a scrapbook showing everything that's gone on at the agency since Fiona started it. You wouldn't believe some of the dusty old boxes I hunted through," she added nervously. "I had everyone working there helping me keep it a secret. There ended up being a, um, a lot of stuff."

His lips tilted. "I'll bet. And she'll love it." Then he leaned toward her. "You take my breath away." His low voice whispered over her ear as his lips brushed her cheek.

She actually felt faint for a moment and stared up at him as he straightened. "How can you tell?" She cleared her throat and tugged her collar. "I'm wearing a coat."

He brushed his thumb over her chin. "Believe me. I can tell. Everything all right?"

Except that she knew she was being dazzled by him? "Fine." She took another sip of her champagne, willing her heart to move back down into her chest where it belonged. "I didn't mean to be this late. I was held up this afternoon having lunch with my mother. Where's Fiona?"

"Being held captive by *my* mother and some guests she's introducing." Gabe took her hand, setting off yet another bout of weak knees as he tucked it around his arm and turned her toward the house. He added her gift to the collection already gathered on a long table and his head lowered again so she could hear his soft voice. "Astrid doesn't seem to recognize the irony in having to introduce someone to Fiona at Fiona's own party."

"Maybe we should mount a rescue," Bobbie suggested just as softly.

Gabe's eyes crinkled. "I knew you were a kindred spirit."

Her smile felt shaky. The man was much too appealing. It was an effort to remind herself that he was still a man with an agenda—even as justified as his cause was.

She had no desire to get burned again, and every speck of self-preservation that she possessed was shrieking at her that she would be in even more deeply over her head where Gabriel Gannon was concerned than she had ever been with Lawrence. And even though she was finally realizing that she hadn't wanted to die of a broken heart when *that* had ended, the experience had still been a humiliating disaster.

Unfortunately, there was also a small voice inside her head that was screaming at her that it was already too late.

Her fingertips pressed against the hard biceps she could feel through the very fine fabric of his exquisitely cut dinner jacket. She tipped the champagne glass to her lips again, swallowing down the last sip of the sparkling wine before depositing the glass on an elegantly draped high-top table near the doorway. "Then what are we waiting for?"

Gabe's smile grew slowly. He covered her hand on his arm with his and squeezed as he escorted her into the house.

Several sets of eyes immediately turned toward them, but Bobbie didn't have a chance to shy away because his hand tightened even more on hers. "Everybody, this—" he looked down at her in a way that had her heart jumping back into her throat all over again "—is Bobbie. She's—"

"—the one renting Fiona's carriage house," one of the cookie-cutter wives put in with a tone that had Bobbie's smile stiffening.

"—a close friend of mine," Gabe continued as if he hadn't been interrupted at all.

"And one of my all-time favorite people." Fiona's voice was as bright as her yellow gown as she swept into the room, giving Bobbie barely enough time to notice the way Gabe's brothers had glanced at each other after his words.

"Bobbie, dear, you've never looked lovelier." Fiona brushed her cheek against Bobbie's before straightening and smiling at her and Gabe. "Give me your coat and let me see your gown. We won't let you freeze. There are heaters going outside."

Bobbie obediently slipped out of her coat and Fiona handed it off to a server she flagged down. "Now," she said with satisfaction, "You two are surely the most striking couple here."

Couple? Bobbie hoped to heaven she didn't look as jarred as she felt hearing the term, particularly hearing it from Gabe's own grandmother.

And the way that Gabe tucked her hand around his arm again didn't help any.

"Grandmother, you're going to hurt our feelings." The same woman who'd set Bobbie's teeth on edge pouted prettily as she snuggled up next to her husband.

Fiona waved her hand dismissively. "Renée, don't worry. We all know you and Diana both have a closet full of beauty pageant crowns."

Renée smiled, evidently mollified.

"Has Gabriel introduced you to everyone?" Fiona tucked her arm through Bobbie's other one, making her feel surrounded by support.

"He was working on it."

"Ah." Fiona gestured to Renée and her husband, a tall man with a sprinkling of gray in his brown hair. "This is Liam and Renée." Liam, Bobbie knew was Gabe's oldest brother. "And Paul and Diana." She gestured to the other couple. "Liam and Paul, of course, are the Gannon part of the Gannon Law

Group, along with their—oh, there he is. Colin." Fiona waited for the tall, silver-haired man to join them. "My son, Colin. Dear, this is Bobbie Fairchild. I've told you about her."

"Of course." Bobbie found herself face to face with Gabe's father and knew she was seeing what the future Gabe would probably look like: silver-haired and incredibly handsome. And his smile was much more natural than either Liam's or Paul's. More like Gabe's, in fact. "I'm glad to finally meet you, Bobbie. I've met your mother, actually. She served on a committee with Astrid several years ago. She's a lovely woman."

"Thank you." Bobbie managed a smile. She still felt rather like a specimen on a pin. "It's nice to meet all of you." She took in the others with her smile.

"And now that the niceties have been observed," Fiona said brightly, "you all go on and have a dance." She waved toward the French doors and the tent outside. "I'm going to see if I can get that band to play something from this century." She headed out.

"I'd better make sure she doesn't cross swords with Astrid again," Colin murmured with a wry smile that reminded Bobbie even more strongly of his youngest son before he strode out the doors. His daughters-in-law were hard on his heels as they prodded Liam and Paul out into the evening.

Which left Bobbie standing there alone with Gabe and she was suddenly very aware that her breast was pressed closely against the arm she was clutching.

She moistened her lips and carefully loosened her grip, stepping a few inches away. "Your family seems nice."

He cocked an eyebrow. "They're judgmental and pretentious and my sisters-in-law care more about how many diamonds they're wearing and how long they can stave off their wrinkles than anything else."

"Gabe!"

His lips tilted. "Don't worry. It's nothing I haven't told them to their faces. And they, in turn, find me as alien as I find them. But we all do care about one thing."

"Fiona?"

"Exactly." He turned her toward him, his hands cupping her shoulders. His thumbs brushed over the sleeves of her gown and her breathing went all scrambled again. "I did tell you how incredible you look, right?"

She nodded. "You—" the word came out sounding like a croak and she winced. "You clean up pretty well yourself. I like the bowtie," she added unwisely. Unwise because what she was thinking wasn't how urbane he looked in his dressy clothing, but how much she wanted to tug that tie apart. To slowly unfasten the mother-of-pearl studs down the front of his white shirt and peel it back—

She blinked and looked out the doors beside them, desperately trying to focus on the reality of the tent, the sparkling lights, the guests...

Anything but her increasingly uncontrolled attraction to him.

"You all right?" His thumbs brushed over her collarbones again. "You're looking flushed."

She was flushed.

From head to toe and every point in between.

Not even Lawrence had had such an effect on her, and she'd actually planned to marry him!

She swallowed and looked up at him. "You haven't given up on the idea of passing me off as your fiancée at all, have you," she accused bluntly.

His gaze didn't waver from her face. "I never claimed that I had."

"You haven't brought it up since the evening at my sister's bistro."

"If I had, you would have said no again. And I wanted to

give you some time to really consider it. Because once you're in, I need you to stay in until the end."

"The end being a satisfactory custody ruling." She didn't wait for a verbal confirmation of what was plain on his face. "I'm not unsympathetic, Gabe. I've seen for myself how much you love your kids." It had been as much an ingredient during their shared dinner the night before as the pizza and lemonades. "And I really do hope you get what you want. For all of your sakes. But surely I'm not the only woman you can ask."

"I told you already. I don't date."

Her hands flopped. "Which I find just as hard to believe now as I did when you said it." She realized her voice had risen, and, flushing, looked guiltily around them. But they were the only ones in the spacious living room with its collection of comfortably feminine sofas and chairs and priceless artwork, probably because outside, the band had actually begun playing something from a recent decade. More people had joined Gabe's brothers and their wives on the dance floor. Nobody was paying Bobbie and Gabe any attention at all.

She lowered her voice anyway. "Maybe you're not dating anyone right this minute—" goodness knew she wasn't either "—but someone you *used* to—" She went silent when he pressed his finger over her mouth.

"If I tell you that I haven't dated anyone since I came to Seattle, will that convince you?"

"But that was a few years ago," she exclaimed, even though he hadn't moved his finger at all.

Which only succeeded in making her lips tingle even more.

"I know that was years ago. Look, I'll admit that there were women—" he grimaced a little "—a lot of women, for a while after Steph and I split. But none of them mattered. And since I've come to Seattle, I've had more important things on my plate." He moved his hand back to her shoulder. His lips twisted wryly. "If that gets me a sympathy vote, I'm not above using it to my advantage, either."

Sympathy wasn't what was curling through her.

"I don't want to mess anything up for you."

His hands tightened. "You won't."

"That's what my fiancé told me," she countered, "and he learned how wrong he was, too."

"You were engaged?"

"*Were* being the operative word."

"When?"

"Nearly a year ago."

"What happened?"

She exhaled. Maybe if he knew, he'd understand. "I was engaged to Lawrence McKay."

His brows pulled together. "He has something to do with the city, doesn't he?"

"He's on the city council, though he has much grander aspirations." At least he had when they were dating.

She stepped away from Gabe's hands, hoping that her mind would function more clearly if he wasn't touching her. But when she stepped backward, her sharp heel caught in her gown and she heard an ominous rip as she tottered backward.

"Whoa." He caught her before she could fall flat on her rear.

"See?" She craned her head around, lifting the back of her gleaming gown to see the torn hem. "This is the kind of stuff that always happens!"

"You catch your heel?"

"Or I spill cherry pie down the front of a white blouse at a fund-raising luncheon, or I laugh too loud, or I don't get a joke when everyone else does. Or I tell the largest supporter of my fiancé's congressional aspirations that he's a hypocrite for publicly criticizing a waterfront project that he's privately investing in!"

"Sounds like he was a hypocrite."

"Which wasn't the point. Lawrence needed a woman by his side who was a credit to him, not someone who hadn't stuck with one job for more than a year at a time and that he was constantly having to find excuses for, or—"

"He sounds like a drip," Gabe said flatly.

Bobbie stared. "That's what Fiona calls him."

"And she's generally right when it comes to summing up people. So what happened after you called the hypocrite a hypocrite?"

She made a face. "Lawrence learned that I wasn't sitting on the trust fund he assumed I'd have."

"Why would he think you had a trust fund?"

"Because my father was Harrison Hunt's partner when he started HuntCom and I'd already donated a…small amount to his campaign." If nearly every dime she'd had left in her savings could be considered small. She rubbed the side of her nose, looking away.

Uncle Harry had given her and her sisters each a hundred thousand dollars when they'd graduated from high school. Bobbie, of course, was the only one who had managed to fritter away the money without accomplishing something brilliant first. Like opening her own restaurant or traveling the world or getting a fancy degree.

"He made the same assumption that a lot of people have, who know about my connection with the Hunts. But my father died when I was little and with expenses and, um, stuff, there wasn't as much left over for us as there might have been. HuntCom didn't really take off until after that."

"And McKay?"

"Broke off the engagement, of course."

"He's an idiot."

"In front of five hundred people attending the fund-raising dinner," she added.

He grimaced. "A drip with no class. Politics is probably the perfect place for him."

An unexpected laugh bubbled out of her lips. "Don't make me laugh. This is serious."

"I can't take anyone seriously who is stupid enough to hurt the person he's supposed to love. But it's my luck that you're free of him now."

She felt unsteady all over again, and it didn't take stepping through the hem of her dress to do it.

All it took was Gabe.

She sternly reminded herself that he wasn't talking about love and forever with *her*.

He was talking about a pretend engagement for the next several weeks for the express purpose of salvaging his right to his own children.

Could she do that?

Help him, while remembering that helping was the *only* thing she was supposed to be doing?

She stared up at him, at his blue eyes, which seemed to hold nothing but sincerity.

"I—"

"Gabriel." The cool, feminine voice cut across Bobbie's words, making her start. "If you're done flirting with the help, I'd like a moment."

Chapter Six

Gabe barely managed to hold back an oath at the sound of his ex-wife's voice.

Bobbie had been about to agree.

It had been as plain as the straight, slightly short nose on her pretty face.

And now, the gaze that had been locked on his face had turned from that soft, warm gray to a panicky silver.

He gave her a smile that he hoped to hell was calmer than he felt, and slid his arm around her shoulder as he turned to face his ex-wife, who'd entered the living room from within the house. Calling Steph on her rudeness would have been as futile as pointing out the same failure in his sisters-in-law.

They just didn't get it.

"What is it, Stephanie? I'm fresh out of flies for you to pull the wings off of."

Her lips thinned as she strolled into the room as if she owned it. Her figure-hugging, sparkling gown was as icy blue as the eyes studying his arm around Bobbie's shoulders. "This is a private matter. Regarding your children."

He felt Bobbie starting to inch away. "I'll leave you alone—"

"No need." He held her close, still watching his ex-wife. "Whatever you have to say, you can say in front of Bobbie."

Stephanie lifted an imperious eyebrow. She didn't even spare Bobbie so much as a glance, and Gabe's jaw tightened until his back teeth felt on edge.

She tossed her white fur wrap carelessly over the arm of a couch. "*This* is the Bobbie person that Toddy mentioned? I thought *he* was a friend of yours."

"As you can see, *she* is. More than a friend."

If anything, his ex-wife's thin lips went even thinner. She walked toward the French doors, looking out for a moment before turning on him. "In that case, I don't appreciate you parading your girlfriends in front of my children when you are *supposed* to be taking care of them."

"We had dinner with Bobbie, Steph. It's not like we got caught romping around in your bed," he added pointedly.

"Gabe," Bobbie murmured beside him. "Really, I should go."

"Yes," Stephanie agreed immediately. "You should. Gabriel needs to be considering *his* children, not making a fool of himself *over* a child."

"You're sinking to depths that are low, even for you, Steph."

"Excuse me." Bobbie moved out from beneath his arm. Her voice was determined. "I'll leave you both alone to discuss whatever it is you need to discuss."

She stopped next to Stephanie, who stood at least six inches taller than her, and Gabe nearly laughed when it looked to him as if she still managed to look down her nose at his ex-wife. "It's been...interesting to meet you, Mrs. Walker. But let me just say that in my experience, Gabe has never done anything where he *didn't* have the best welfare of his children in mind."

Then she looked back at him, and there were flags of color in her cheeks. "Which is one of the reasons why I think he's going to be a wonderful husband." She smiled at him before turning on her heel and sweeping past Stephanie through the French doors.

He watched her sail across the terrace. She looked so purposeful that it was hardly even noticeable that she was holding up the side of her dress in her hand to keep the torn hem from dragging behind her.

He didn't know if he was more stunned by Bobbie's in-your-face announcement of their intentions, or in awe.

"Don't tell me you're planning to actually marry that girl." Stephanie recovered more quickly than he, and her tone was more acidic than ever. "She's not even in *your* class…such as it is."

Gabe rounded on her. "What is your problem, Steph? I'm used to you flinging everything I do around in the mud, but you usually keep that nastiness reserved just for me. I wonder how your husband would feel knowing you insulted a woman that Harrison Hunt considers almost family?"

"What are you talking about?"

"Bobbie Fairchild." He knew that Stephanie wouldn't give a fig that Bobbie was very dear to Fiona, because Stephanie didn't care in the least about Fiona. But he knew what Stephanie did care about.

The same thing she'd always cared about.

Her husband and his high-paying career as one of Hunt-Com's legal eagles.

"She knows Harrison Hunt *very* well," he finished.

His ex-wife paled and he knew the dart had finally hit home.

She glanced outside, probably spotting Bobbie's distinct

head of curls among the guests as easily as he did. "That... girl...knows Mr. Hunt?"

Gabe smiled coldly. "More than knows him. Family friends. She even calls him Uncle Harry."

"Ethan doesn't answer to Mr. Hunt. He works for *Grayson* Hunt." Her chin had lifted, but there was still a wariness in her voice that—if he were a forgiving sort—would have made him feel some regret over having put there.

Only he wasn't the forgiving sort.

"But they're all one big happy family, aren't they? Isn't that one of the things Ethan's talked about? How the Hunts keep the power to themselves? An international company the size of HuntCom...and it's all privately held by Harrison Hunt and his family."

"Fine," she snapped. "I'll...apologize to her."

"I thought you might. Nothing can ever get in the way of dear Ethan's career. Where is he, by the way?"

"Still in D.C. and he's worked hard to get where he is."

That, actually, was something that Gabe didn't dispute. Didn't make him love the guy any, but there was no denying the man's success. Or that he'd been generous with the results when it came to Lisette and Todd. They had the best of everything.

But that, too, made Gabe's fight that much steeper.

"I still don't believe you really intend to marry her." Evidently, Steph couldn't leave well enough alone. "You don't even believe in marriage. You swore you'd never make that mistake again."

"You know what they say about the wonders of the right woman."

Her glare would have done Medusa proud. "So when is the happy day?"

"We wanted to wait until after Fiona's party and tell the kids before announcing it officially." The lies came so easily he wondered if he was all that different than his brothers after all. Neither one of them took a truthful track if they could accomplish more with a lie. "We haven't set a date yet. Bobbie's never been married, and I want her to have the wedding of her dreams."

At that, his ex-wife finally looked away, and the compunction that Gabe hadn't been able to feel earlier crept in anyway. She and Gabe had eloped. And Gabe knew her wedding with Ethan had been even more hurried. He'd been surprised that she hadn't turned up pregnant shortly after, since that was the only reason she'd been willing to forgo a traditional, all-the-trimmings wedding with Gabe. She hadn't wanted her unplanned pregnancy to show while walking down the aisle in a fancy wedding gown.

"How nice for her," she said stiffly. "If you'll excuse me, I haven't managed to give my birthday wishes to Fiona yet." She grabbed up her wrap.

He exhaled tiredly. Even before their divorce, they'd traded more jabs than anything else, and after years of sniping, he was heartily sick of the habit. The only good things that had resulted from their union had been Lisette and Todd. It would be nice if they could stop battling over them, too, though he couldn't see that ever happening when Stephanie considered his effort to gain joint custody tantamount to stealing them completely. "What was it about the kids you wanted to discuss?"

She slid the fur around her shoulders. "Todd's school counselor wants to have another meeting with us on Wednesday to discuss moving him to a different math class."

"You mean *you* want to have another meeting." They'd been arguing the subject for a month.

"I don't want Toddy feeling like a failure if I let them move him to an easier math class," Stephanie said.

Gabe shook his head. "He won't. And neither should you." Which was the real crux of the problem, he was certain.

"As if," she sniffed. "Just because you always choose the easy way out doesn't mean I want my son learning to do so."

He almost laughed. The easy way in the Gannon family meant following the same pattern. Which he hadn't done, in spades.

But Stephanie knew that he agreed with the counselor, who not only insisted that both of Todd's parents be included in their sessions, but believed that moving the boy to a class more suited to his skills would help him gain the confidence he needed in order to excel. Unfortunately, what Gabe thought didn't "officially" matter, since Stephanie had the legal right to make such decisions.

Which had left them at an impasse for too long. And Todd was the one suffering for it.

"Let me know what time the meeting is, and I'll be there."

She didn't look particularly mollified, but then he hadn't expected her to. "And Lisette has a dance recital Thursday evening. She insisted that I remind you, even though I warned her you would be too busy for that, too."

"I'm not too busy for either Todd or Lisette."

"Only for your wife," she countered. "Perhaps having a friendly chat with Bobbie won't be so difficult after all. I should probably warn her what she's getting herself into. Woman to woman, and all."

"Stay away from Bobbie."

"I thought I was supposed to apologize to her."

"I've changed my mind. Your apologies are too similar to poisonous apples."

Stephanie laughed coolly. "You always did have such a charming way with words." Assured of having the last say, she moved out onto the terrace and he heard her voice above the music. "Renée, honey. How long has it been? A year? Two! You look fabulous."

He let out a breath as her voice faded. God, he was glad that she was gone.

"Hey." Bobbie appeared in the same doorway that Stephanie had come from to interrupt them. "Is the coast clear?"

He wondered how much she'd overheard, then decided it really didn't matter. Before all was said and done, she would probably hear plenty of verbal sword fighting between him and Stephanie, and be glad to wash her hands of all of them. "It's clear."

"Good. I've been hiding out in the kitchen for the last ten minutes." She lifted her hands and he realized she was holding two bottles of beer. "Want one?"

Almost more than his next breath. He took the cold bottle from her. "Where'd you find these?"

"Fiona's fridge." She grinned, though her expression wasn't entirely easy. "The bar that your mother arranged has everything under the sun from pinot grigio to limoncello and all things in between, but no beer."

"Not surprising. Astrid considers any beer—" he glanced at the label on the bottle "—even local brews like this, an inferior breed." He eyed her. "I'm sorry."

"For what?"

"Need you ask? The charming delight that is my former wife."

"She's hardly the first person to think I am an inferior breed." She lifted her shoulder and took a sip of her beer. A tiny jeweled flower sparkled amongst her rioting spirals of hair. "Besides. You're not responsible for what she says."

He rolled the cold beer against his palm, cooling the itch to touch those shining curls. "Unfortunately, that's not necessarily true."

She looked up at him and for a blinding second, he nearly forgot what he intended to say. But then her smooth eyebrows quirked together a little over her nose, and he dragged himself out of the warmth of her gaze.

"I'm the one who brings out the worst in her," he finally admitted. "I made her miserable during the few years we were married, and she's never forgotten it. And *you* are anything but inferior. I don't know how I'm going to be able to thank you."

"You don't have to." She held his gaze for a moment, then her lashes swept down as she took another sip of her beer.

He cleared his throat and focused on his own beer bottle. It was safer. "I told her that we wanted to wait until after the party was over to announce it, but word's probably going to get around pretty quickly anyway," he said after a moment. "Discretion has never been one of Stephanie's strong suits."

She nodded. Another little sparkle in her hair flashed in the light. "Fiona's not going to be fooled. And what about your children? What are you going to tell them?"

"I'm not worried about my grandmother. She's always on my side." He knew it unequivocally. She was the only one in his family who never wavered in that regard. "As for my kids, I'll tell them only as much as I need to."

She frowned. "We'll be lying to them, too."

He'd already realized that. "It can't be helped. It's not as if I can give them the real scoop." And fortunately he knew his ex-wife wouldn't be in any hurry to tell them, either. She'd figure that announcing an engagement would be his problem.

"I suppose it's also probably too much to hope for that word won't get back to *my* family somehow. The city sometimes feels ridiculously small. You never know who knows who. I'm not going to lie to my mother, though. Or my sisters. They are discreet. So don't worry about that."

"I'm not worried about your family. But there's something I

need to tell you before it comes back and bites me on the butt. Something that I probably should have told you before."

She gave him a sideways glance. "That sounds ominous."

"It's not important to me. But it just goes to prove that you're right. The city is small." And he hadn't told her yet that she wasn't the only one in this mess who had a connection to Harrison Hunt, though his was a whole lot less important.

He glanced outside. Now that the music was more lively, none of the partygoers were looking their direction, much less approaching the house. "Ethan—the guy trying to raise my kids like they're his own—works for HuntCom."

As she absorbed that, her eyes visibly cooled. "I...see."

Her expression, combined with the itch at the back of his neck, assured him that she undoubtedly didn't. At least not from his point of view. "He's in their legal department."

"What do you want me to do about that?" She set her beer carefully on an antique side table. "Dial up Uncle Harry and ask him to fire Ethan so there's no European job at all? Seems to me that would have been a better plan on your part than trying to pull one over on the judge in your custody battle."

Coming on the heels of the unpleasantness with Stephanie, her assessment bit like sharp, pointed teeth. "I would never put you in that position," he said slowly. Truthfully.

He set down his own beer, taking the time to let that quick shard of anger inside him dull. "But that's the second time you've jumped to the conclusion that I wanted something from you specifically because of your association with Hunt. I'll tell you the same thing I told you before. I'm not interested in HuntCom or trying to use your connection there to my advantage." He didn't count using it to stop his ex-wife from bad-mouthing Bobbie behind her back. "Just because that's what people have wanted from you in the past doesn't mean that's what I want. The only reason I'm even bringing it up now is because I didn't want you hearing it from someone else and starting to think exactly what you're thinking."

"So you could have told me before. When you first learned about Uncle Harry."

"I was wrong, all right? You deserved full disclosure right from the start, but frankly, I was more interested in convincing you to help me follow my attorney's advice!" At least as much of the advice as Gabe could stand to follow. "It wouldn't matter to me if you'd never *heard* of Harrison Hunt."

He exhaled and found another store of patience from some place that he didn't even know existed.

She was standing there so stiffly in her pretty, torn gown, as if she were braced for the inevitable worst, and just then he wanted to string up everyone from their thumbs who'd ever put such doubt in her.

"Bobbie," he began again, more calmly. "I'm a simple man. I build things. I don't go around manipulating people and situations. I'm just trying to hold onto my kids. Despite your suspicions that nobody could possibly want something from you simply because you are *you,* I'm telling you the truth. I just need you to help me level the playing field when I get to court."

She chewed her lower lip. "I work in a coffee shop, Gabe. I can barely pay my own bills. How on earth is that going to provide any sort of leveling?"

"Not everything is about money." He could almost hear the Gannon family collectively gasping. "And I'm not exactly standing in the welfare lines. A lot of what I have is tied up in the company, but that doesn't mean I can't provide just as well for my children as Stephanie does, courtesy of her husband's billable hours." It would just take a helluva lot larger chunk of his income, but he'd deal with it.

"If you're going to change your mind about all this, then let me know now," he added, "because the closer we get to the hearing, the worse it'll be if you do. I'm trying to prove my stability and now that Steph thinks we're engaged, if we turn out suddenly not to be right before we go to court, she'll try using that to her advantage."

Bobbie pushed her fingers through her hair, holding the mass of long curls away from her heart-shaped face. She closed her gray eyes and shook her head a little. Her dark hair slid in curling ribbons against her pale skin. "I'm not going to change my mind." She opened her eyes again, dropping her hands. A smile that struck him as oddly sad played around her soft lips. "In it until the end, and all that, right?"

He didn't even realize how much he'd been afraid she would reconsider until the relief hit him after her words. "Right." His throat felt unaccountably tight.

"Do me a favor? While we're pretending for everyone else, don't pretend with me. Custody of your children is so much more important than me ruining some stupid fund-raising dinner for a jerk. If you think I'm becoming a hindrance, you have to tell me, so—"

He caught her face in his hands and her eyes went wide as her voice trailed off. "Have a little faith in yourself, Bobbie. I do."

She blinked, looking startled, and moistened her lips. "I'll...try."

"Good." He realized he was staring at her glistening lower lip and made himself drop his hands. "Good," he said again and picked up his beer to wash down the gruffness in his throat. "Now that we've got that straightened out, maybe we should go join the party. Do you want to dance?" She was young and beautiful. Of course she'd want to dance. And he wasn't hypocritical enough to deny that putting his arms around her for the few measures of a song was an appealing notion.

"I'm not much good at it." She lifted her skirt a few inches, smiling wryly. "My coordination only seems to come together when I'm playing sports."

"What about yoga?"

"Well." She tilted her hand back and forth, suddenly looking discomfited. "I guess I do passably well. Sometimes."

He knew only too well that she'd looked more than passably sexy in her yoga getup. He took another pull of cold beer, willing his body back into order. "That leaves a lot of other sports still. Tiddlywinks. Boxing."

The dimple in her cheek appeared. "Neither, I'm afraid." She shrugged, looking more at ease. "I like golf and softball. Volleyball. Basketball was a no-go for obvious reasons." She waved her hand at herself. "I did run track in school, though. High jump. Hurdles. Relay."

All of which required plenty of coordination. "Discus," he offered.

"Ah." Her smile broadened suddenly, mischievously. "Discobolos. The Discus Thrower." Her gaze ran down his body as if she were comparing him to Myron's famous Greek sculpture. "I can imagine that."

The heat running up his spine might have been embarrassment. It was more likely knowing she was comparing him to a naked statue and, judging by her expression, he wasn't faring too badly.

He let out a laugh aimed more at himself than anything and drank down the rest of the beer. This is what he got for spending months—years—focused on things more important than his sex life. Now it was an effort to think about anything else.

"Outside," he suggested. The chilly night air would have to suffice since a cold shower wasn't available as long as he was at Fiona's.

She nodded and headed for the doorway. Her chin ducked for a moment, but not quickly enough to hide her flushed cheeks from him. "Maybe Fiona will open her gifts soon and we can go home." She didn't wait for him, but hurried outside, still holding her torn skirt off to the side.

He let out a long, long breath and started to follow. But a sparkle on the carpet caught his attention and he bent down to pick it up.

A tiny, faceted daisy winked up at him.

Smiling slightly, he slipped the hairpin into his pocket and followed Bobbie into the night.

Fiona, they soon found, was not even remotely close to opening her gifts. Even though his grandmother had complained loudly about the party, she was the one in the center of the dance floor cutting a rug with Gabe's father.

Gabe stood behind Bobbie, where she'd stopped to watch from the edge of the crowded dance floor. It was even more crowded around the wooden square, though, which was his only excuse for standing so close to her that he could smell that hint of lemony freshness in her hair. And when a couple brushed against them as they sidled through to the dance floor, it was only natural for Gabe to slide his arm around Bobbie's waist to keep her from being knocked sideways.

She looked up at him and her eyes seemed darker, more like the smoky color of her dress in the soft light from the twinkling strands circling the tent above their heads. "Thanks."

He managed a nod. He could feel the natural curve of her waist beneath the smooth, silky fabric of her gown.

"Fiona and your father are putting everyone else to shame."

He nodded again, making himself look away from her face. On the opposite side of the dance floor, he could see his mother standing arm-in-arm with Stephanie. Fortunately, both of them seemed more interested in whatever they were talking about—most likely the spectacle Fiona was making of herself as she swung around with abandon to a song he was pretty sure Lisette listened to on her MP3 player—than in paying him any heed.

Barely a few minutes had passed when the pounding song ended, though, giving way to a slower beat. He could hear his grandmother's breathless laughter amid the small exodus from the dance floor.

He leaned down so Bobbie would hear. "This is more my speed. You game?" His arm was still wrapped around her waist and he felt her quick inhale.

"I suppose I can't do more damage to my dress than I've already done." She gave a little turn right out from beneath his arm, then caught his hand in hers as she stepped off the grass onto the dance floor.

Fiona passed by them, smiling benevolently. "That's what I've been waiting to see." She patted their arms before stepping off the dance floor. "Where's that boy with the cocktails?" he heard her asking.

"I hope I'm as fabulous as she is when I'm her age." Bobbie stepped into his arms, though her gaze seemed carefully fixed on Fiona's movements.

"You're pretty fabulous now." God knew she felt fabulous. He'd have to be dead not to know it. And lately, since he'd met her, he was feeling more alive than he had in years.

Her lips curving, she looked up at him through the dark fringe of her eyelashes. "You're just saying that because I've fallen in with your plans."

They were barely shuffling around on the crowded dance floor. He tucked his knuckle beneath her softly pointed chin and nudged it upward.

Her playful smile slowly died as he looked into her wide eyes. "I'm saying it because it's true."

"Gabe—" Her soft voice broke off.

He'd never before thought his thumb had a mind of its

own, but evidently it did, brushing across the fullness of her lower lip.

Her gaze flickered. "Let's not forget what we're really doing here."

His left hand seemed damnably independent, too, sliding more firmly around her back, drawing her silk-draped curves even closer against him. "What I'm really doing," he murmured in her ear, "is trying not to kiss you right now."

Her head went back a little further. Her long, spiraling curls tickled his fingers pressing against her spine. "Really?"

"Don't be surprised," he reminded. "You started it." His lips closed over hers.

That quick inhale. That faint little *mmming* sound of delight. It burned through him as suddenly as the flare of a match. Only this flame wasn't going to burn itself out quickly…or easily. Just then, as unwise as he knew it was, he didn't care. His fingertips pressed into the smooth arch of her back and he felt her hands sliding up his chest, over his shoulders—

"Oh. I'm so sorry!"

Gabe barely heard the exclamation, but Bobbie yanked back from him. "It's not your fault," he heard her breathless assurance.

Feeling half-witted, he realized the woman dancing behind them had stepped on Bobbie's dress that she'd forgotten to hold up, making the tear ten times worse, and ten times more noticeable.

Her face was flushed and she didn't meet his eyes when she turned back toward him. "I have to go."

"It's just a tear—"

"I know." She was already backing away from him. Physically and mentally. "But I, um, I should do something about it." Her lips stretched. "Fortunately, I don't have to go far."

"I'll come with you."

"No!" She shook her head. "Stay. Fiona will miss you. I'll just...later. We'll...later."

Nonsensical, but perfectly meaningful.

She looked panicked.

So he shoved his hands in his pockets to keep them from getting any more ideas, and let her go. "All right."

She barely hesitated before hurrying from beneath the warmth and light of the tent. He watched her as she practically ran in her high heels and flapping hem across the lawn and down the slight hill toward her carriage house.

She might as well have been Cinderella on the run.

Inside his pocket, he rolled her tiny, sharp-edged hair clip between his fingers.

Unfortunately, in this fairy tale, he knew he was no prince.

Not when he'd long ago stopped believing in happily-ever-afters.

Chapter Seven

"So, how was the birthday party last night?" Bobbie's sister Tommi, looking flushed from the heat of the kitchen, flicked open the top few buttons of her white chef's jacket and sat down on one of the barstools next to where Bobbie was sitting, filling salt shakers. It was the only "payment" Tommi would accept for the delicious crab bisque and baguettes that Bobbie had scarfed down for lunch.

The afternoon shift was over, the waitstaff and last of the customers departed, and this being Monday, Tommi wouldn't be reopening in a few hours again for dinner like on the other days of the week. "It was okay. I didn't stay all that long, actually." Bobbie focused hard on not letting the plastic funnel overflow. "Aside from Fiona, I didn't really know anyone."

"Wasn't her Mr. Handyman grandson there?"

Bobbie nodded casually. "Gabe? Sure. Of course. Most of Fiona's family were there."

Tommi's fingertips slowly drummed the bar's surface. "So...?"

There was never any fooling the Fairchild women. Not their mother, Cornelia, nor Cornelia's daughters.

But Bobbie could still try. She'd warned Gabe that she wouldn't lie to her family. And even though she knew it would be better to tell them herself than chance them hearing about their "engagement" through gossip, she still couldn't summon any enthusiasm for admitting to them what she'd agreed to. No matter what the reason, none of them would approve of her participation in something deceitful.

"So...nothing." Bobbie tucked her tongue between her teeth, moving the salt shaker to the trio of filled ones before sliding another in its place. She glanced at her sister's tired face. "I wish you'd hire another sous chef," she said. The guy who'd held the position had been gone for over a month now. "This place has gotten way too busy for you to handle everything alone."

Tommi just shrugged. "We'll see. Finding the right person isn't all that easy. Is there something going on between you and Gabe?"

Bobbie scattered salt across the bar before quickly redirecting the funnel. "Why would you think that?"

Tommi smoothly scooped the salt off the black granite and into the tall, empty coffee cup from Between the Bean that Bobbie had left sitting beside her. "Maybe the fact that you can't say the man's name without looking flushed."

"What can I say? I'm still not exactly proud of the way I attacked his lips the day we met." Tommi knew about that episode but Bobbie hadn't admitted that any more lip-locking had occurred—instigated by either one of them.

"Fair enough. Except you've also now filled four salt shakers with sugar. Which is pretty odd even for you, so I'm thinking there's still something on your mind."

Bobbie blinked. She looked down at the plastic container she'd grabbed from Tommi's shelves and groaned. The label on it did say *sugar*.

She dumped the funnel's contents back into the container. "Some help I am, huh?" She slid off the black barstool, heading toward the narrow swinging doors that led to the kitchen. "I'll fix it."

But Tommi caught her by the cowl neck of her orange sweater, halting her escape. "The salt can wait. What's really going on? You've never been this preoccupied, not even when you were in the throes of infatuation for Larry-the-political-dweeb."

Bobbie tugged her collar free. "It's complicated."

"Why? Because he's too old for you?"

"He is not!"

Tommi gave her a serenely patient smile. "I *knew* you were interested in him," she said with the superiority of a year-older sister.

Bobbie exhaled. "Fat lot of good it will do me," she muttered. She picked up the sugar container. "He's not exactly long-term material," she said before pushing through the swinging doors. She slid the heavy container back into its spot on the orderly dry goods shelves and retrieved the one marked *salt* instead. She also grabbed four empty salt shakers from storage and when she carried everything back out to the wine bar, Tommi was tipping the incorrect contents into the empty coffee cup.

"I'm going to take it as a sign that you've realized Lawrence was all wrong for you, considering the words *long* and *term* have even reentered your vocabulary."

Bobbie slid onto the barstool again. "Maybe," she allowed. "Doesn't make it any less humiliating the way he dumped me."

"He has no class."

"Gabe said that, too."

Tommi's dark eyes sparkled. "Ah. I'm liking him more and more."

Bobbie couldn't help but smile. "You would like him," she said after a moment. "He's a good man. Works hard." She looked down at the large plastic container, but in her mind all she could see was his handsome face. "And there's nothing he won't do for his kids."

Tommi fit the caps back on the salt shakers and pushed them to one side before reaching for the fresh ones Bobbie had brought out from the kitchen. "There are two, right?"

"Mmm-hmm." She propped her elbows on the bar, resting her chin on her hands. "Lisette and Todd. She's twelve and I'm not sure which she's more passionate about—ballet or rap music. Which isn't exactly the music Gabe wants her listening to, but he definitely knows he has to pick his battles where she's concerned. And Todd's ten and so much smarter than he realizes. Honestly, the boy's a whiz when it comes to computers." She smiled to herself. "He ought to be in Hunt-Com's research and development department."

Tommi reached over and pulled the lid off the salt container when Bobbie didn't make any move to. She scooped out a portion to fill the funnel. "Gabe doesn't have them full-time?"

"No, but not for lack of trying. Last week he had them for several days, though. Their mother was out of town." Her lips twisted when she thought of Gabe's former wife. The woman had stood at least five inches taller than Bobbie and she'd worn her self-confidence as easily as she had the numbingly sophisticated gown that had shown off her impeccable figure to its best advantage. "She was at the party, too."

Tommi's smooth motions as she filled the shakers came to a brief pause. "His ex-wife was at Fiona's birthday party? How...well-adjusted."

Bobbie let out a soft snort. "Not exactly." She filled her sister in on Gabe's mother's connection to Stephanie. "His ex and her husband are planning to move outside the country again and take the kids, naturally. Gabe's trying to get their custody arrangement changed so he'll be able to spend more time with the kids, keep them with him for at least part of the year."

"That sounds fairly admirable of him. Seems like there are a lot of men around these days who would happily leave the responsibility to someone else." With the spare efficiency that came with long practice, Tommi capped the shakers and gathered them all up in her hands to take around to the tables that had already been draped with fresh, white linens for the next day. "But you think Gabe's not long-term material."

Bobbie twisted around on her stool, watching Tommi. "He says he's not," she corrected. "Can't get much plainer than that."

"Not unless he packs up and leaves, I suppose," Tommi agreed. Finished with her task, she moved to the large front window that was stenciled in gold with *The Corner Bistro* and looked out on the rain-drenched street. "Hard to believe it's going to be Christmas in a couple of months," she murmured. "Your Gabe sounds like a man who comes with a closetful of baggage."

Bobbie bristled. "Which means what, exactly?"

Tommi glanced over her shoulder. "Meaning just that, sis. You said yourself it was complicated. You don't have to get defensive."

Bobbie exhaled and deliberately relaxed her shoulders. "Well, the complications get even more twisted."

From across the cozy bistro, she saw her sister's smooth brown eyebrows lift warily. "How…twisted?"

Bobbie wrapped her fingers around the sides of the seat beneath her. "Some people at the party might think I'm engaged to marry him," she admitted slowly.

Tommi's hands lifted. "Why would they think that?"

"Because-I-told-his-ex-wife-we-were."

There. She'd admitted it.

Which still didn't make her own behavior feel any more real.

Her sister put a hand to her head, released the clip holding her smooth, dark hair up in the back and thrust her fingers through the strands as if she'd developed a sudden headache. She pulled out the nearest chair and sat down.

Bobbie picked at a tiny jag in her thumbnail. "And Gabe figures she's not likely to keep the news to herself," she added more slowly.

"Bobbie."

Her shoulders hunched again, even though she tried to stop them. "I told you it was complicated."

"Why don't you start at the beginning and un-complicate it for me, then."

So Bobbie did. Skirting a few of the more intimate details—like how she'd been dissolving from the inside out when she'd danced with Gabe beneath the tent's twinkling lights or how she'd known that if he'd disregarded her words and followed her anyway when she'd left, she would have invited him in for a whole lot more than coffee and a goodnight kiss—she told her sister everything.

And when she was finished, she didn't know if she felt more exhausted or relieved. "I promised him that all of you would have our backs."

Tommi gave a half a laugh, though she didn't sound amused. "Who would I know to tell otherwise?"

"Ethan—that's Stephanie's current husband—works for HuntCom," Bobbie reminded her. "Not that I think Uncle

Harry would care about any of this, but I guess I wouldn't want to chance it. He's not exactly predictable."

"And if you want to look at the money and the board seats he gave us in this particular light, you could say he's been known to be protective of us."

"Right." Bobbie brushed her hands down the thighs of her blue jeans and pushed off the barstool. "I do want to help Gabe—he *really* loves those kids, Tom—but I would hate for someone's career to be jeopardized. Even if he is married to the first cousin of the Wicked Witch."

"There's no earthly reason why Uncle Harry would ever learn about any of this from me." Tommi's voice turned brisk. "I haven't talked to him in weeks. I'm certainly not going to tell him."

"What if Mom does?"

"She wouldn't for the same reasons. Are you clear on the reasons why *you're* doing this?"

"I'm just helping Fiona's grandson," Bobbie insisted. "I know it's not going to lead anywhere…permanent." But she also couldn't stop from wishing otherwise.

"I know Fiona means a lot to you." Her sister grimaced wryly. "But I can also see a look in your eyes when you talk about Gabe that doesn't have anything to do with his grandmother. So just…watch yourself, okay?"

"I'm not under any illusions," she assured. Having her sister's support went a long way toward settling the nerves inside her. "Now, since I didn't even fill any salt shakers, I owe you for the therapy session *and* the lunch."

Tommi smiled again, this time for real. "And when have you ever paid for lunch before?"

Bobbie laughed. They both knew that Tommi would have refused to take her money even if she'd offered it. "Well is there something else I can do around here to help you out?"

Tommi shook her head. "I'm going to catch up on the books a little and then call it a day myself."

"Good." Bobbie retrieved her hooded jacket from where she'd dumped it at the end of the wine bar and slid her arms into it. "You look like you need a long bath and a tall glass of one of those Italian wines you like." She leaned over and hugged her sister, who was still sitting near the front door. "And hire another sous chef, already, so you don't have to work so hard."

Tommi hugged her back. "You work on straightening out your own life and leave me to worry about the bistro," she advised lightly. "What are you dressing up as for Halloween at the Bean tomorrow?" The coffee shop's employees always dressed in costumes for the holiday.

Bobbie lifted her shoulders. "I haven't thought about it much." She'd been more than a little preoccupied of late, though the kids had brought up the issue when they'd been at her house. Their mother considered trick-or-treating too déclassé, but they were planning to dress up for school, though neither child had been particularly enthusiastic about their store-bought costumes.

Tommi looked surprised. And Bobbie couldn't blame her. Since she'd been a girl, she'd always enjoyed putting thought and effort into her Halloween costumes. Even when she had nothing else to do on the day but answer the door and hand out sweets to the children who came knocking. "Aren't you working?"

"Yeah. I've got the morning shift all this week." Even though she usually came and went through the restaurant's back door, she flipped open the lock on the brass-trimmed front glass door. It was pouring, and she had managed to find a coveted street parking spot down the block, which meant leaving through the front door was quicker. "I'll figure out something."

"Go as a bride," Tommi suggested.

"Ha ha." But she managed to laugh, too, as she left her sister to lock up behind her.

When she got home, she let the dogs outside. They loved to play in the rain, so she put them on their chains and left them to it while she went to her closet to find some inspiration for a Halloween costume.

When her phone rang a little while later, she very nearly ignored it, since the only one to call her lately had been Quentin Rich. But it kept ringing and ringing, so she pushed herself off the floor of her closet and went to the phone.

"Bobbie? This is Cheryl. I've been trying to reach you for hours."

Cheryl was Fiona's secretary at the agency. "What's wrong?"

"Fiona. She collapsed in the middle of a meeting over at Cragmin's a few hours ago."

Bobbie's knees went out and she sank onto the corner of her bed. "Is she all right? Where's she now? Does her family know?" *Does Gabe?*

"I reached Mr. Gannon at the law office." Cheryl named the hospital that Fiona had been taken to. "But I don't know what to do about the agency. Everyone here is asking what to do. We have a class of dogs that are supposed to graduate this weekend, and I know she also hasn't finished payroll. Nobody knows what to do!"

Bobbie exhaled. "Keep doing what you normally do," she said simply. "Aaron's the head trainer. He knows what to do for the graduation. The match list of the recipients for the dogs is already done; I saw it on Fiona's credenza when I was there the other day." They would all be present at the training graduation, when the dogs were handed over to their new partners.

"Should I call in someone to do the payroll, or what?"

Cheryl sounded only slightly less frantic. "I hate to even bring it up, but none of us can afford to miss a check. And I obviously can't go asking Mr. Gannon about it now."

"I'll think of something, Cheryl." Though she didn't know what. The office would be closing in little more than an hour. "Don't worry. Just tell everyone to keep doing their jobs. I'll get back to you before the end of the day. Okay?"

"Okay." The other woman hung up, sounding somewhat less frantic. Bobbie, on the other hand, felt like her stomach had been tied into a knot. She called the dogs in and re-crated them with fresh food and water. "Your wet coats are going to have to wait this time," she told them as she added fresh towels to the floor of their cage for them to lie on. As soon as they were settled, she was out the door again, heading to the hospital.

She'd barely gotten off the freeway when her cell phone rang. Not even glancing at where it sat on her console, she thumbed the speaker button and braked behind the long line of cars at a stop light. "Hello?"

"It's Gabe." His deep voice came through loud and clear on the little phone.

"Gabe!" She tightened her hands around the steering wheel. "I'm on my way to the hospital. How is she? How are *you?*"

"She's going to be fine," he said quickly. "I guess I don't have to ask if you heard."

Thank you, thank you, thank you.

"Fiona's secretary called me." She inched forward in traffic while one portion of her mind considered alternate routes. "What happened?"

"She had a mild heart attack."

Bobbie sank her teeth into her tongue to keep them from chattering. She still remembered Harry's heart attack from a few years ago. And her father had died of one.

She'd just seen Fiona the evening before, dancing the night away in her yellow gown.

"Bobbie? Did you hear me?"

She nodded. Foolish. He couldn't see her. "I heard." She swallowed past the knot in her throat again. "How mild?"

"If everything goes well, she should be out of the hospital by the end of the week."

"That's good." She took advantage of a break in traffic to change lanes, turning down a side street. She'd make faster time going through the neighborhoods than on the main streets that were clogged with construction and rush-hour traffic. "Is everyone there?"

"Yeah. Fiona wants to see you."

She had to slow down for a school zone. "I'd have been there by now if not for this damn traffic."

"You're fine," he assured. "She's having some tests run right now, anyway."

"You're sure she's all right?"

"Talked to the doctor myself. Obviously there are some things he wants her to watch, but she got immediate medical attention when it happened and the damage to her heart was minimal." She heard a rustling and then his voice was less clear. "She thinks we're *really* engaged."

Bobbie glanced down at the phone as if she could see Gabe's face. "What?"

"Stephanie told Renée, who told Astrid, who naturally told Fiona."

Her fingers flexed around the steering wheel again. "That wouldn't have caused her—"

"No," he cut her off. "That I can promise you. I left the party shortly after you did, but Fiona evidently knew last night. She told me just a little while ago that she had no intentions of going anywhere before she had the pleasure of seeing us walking down the aisle."

"I *knew* this would blow up in our faces! Didn't I tell you it was a bad idea?"

"Don't panic. Everything will be fine. I just wanted you to know what she was thinking before you see her."

"She should know better than anyone that we haven't been involved."

"Yeah, well, I guess we were wrong in thinking that. From what she's said to me, she takes full credit for putting us together in the first place. I'll tell her the truth when I have to, but not until she's stronger and well again."

"Of course." The last thing Bobbie wanted was to upset Fiona in any way. She turned down another block and could see the tall lines of the hospital building in the distance. "Have you told Lisette and Todd about Fiona?"

"Stephanie did. She brought them to the hospital about a half hour ago."

"Is she still there?" The thought of encountering Gabe's ex-wife again so soon wasn't palatable, but it also wasn't enough to keep her from going to see Fiona.

"She has to leave soon to get ready for some business dinner Ethan's got. She had a sitter lined up for them, but the kids don't want to leave."

"Can you blame them?"

"I don't," he assured mildly. "Getting their mother to agree is another matter, and Fiona doesn't need to hear us arguing about it now."

"Of course not." She turned another corner and nosed her way back onto the main street. The entrance to the hospital was fifty yards away. "I'll be there in a minute. Are you all in the emergency room?"

"She's already been moved to a private room." He told her the number. "It's a little crowded up here, though, so I'll just meet you downstairs by the main entrance." He didn't wait for an answer before he hung up.

Bobbie thumbed the end button on her phone and turned in to the parking lot. There were a half-dozen signs directing people to various areas and she found herself heading up the emergency ramp instead of entering the visitor's parking lot. Cursing under her breath, she turned around at the first opportunity and managed to get herself back where she belonged.

The parking lot was crowded there, too, and she had to park some distance from the entrance, which meant that several minutes had passed before she finally made her way through the automatically sliding doors.

She spotted Gabe right away. He was the tall, broad man in blue jeans and a gray flannel shirt swooping down on her, pulling her into a fierce hug despite the water clinging to her raincoat.

Her heart jumped into her throat as she wrapped her arms around his shoulders. When she stood on her toes, her nose found a spot in the warm crook of his neck. "You told me she's going to be fine," she reminded him huskily.

He nodded and she felt a deep breath work through his chest. Then he was pulling back a little. Enough to press a hard, fast kiss to her lips. "I'm glad you came."

Quick or not, she still felt absurdly rocked by the kiss. "Of course I came."

"For Fiona?" His voice was low.

She pressed her tingling lips together for a moment. "Yes." Telling him she'd been concerned for him, too, would be as good as admitting how quickly she was getting in over her head with him. But she still couldn't prevent her hands from rubbing over his bunched shoulders. He could reassure her that his grandmother was going to be fine, but he was clearly still stressed. "How long have you been here?"

"A few hours. Dad called as soon as he heard. I was on my way out to a job site in Ballard and just turned around to come here. I called your house, but didn't want to leave the news on your answering machine. Would have called your cell sooner, but I didn't know your number until I got hold of Fiona's phone."

She grimaced. What believable couple wouldn't know the phone numbers of their beloved? "How many more things like that should we have thought of?"

"It doesn't matter. I have it now. And you have mine." He tucked her head beneath his chin.

She closed her eyes, breathing in the warmth and comfort of him. "How long do you think it'll be before I can see her?"

"Shouldn't be long." His chest expanded beneath her cheek. "We can go up to her room if you're ready."

She wasn't sure she was, but she nodded anyway. He waited while she slid out of her raincoat, then took her hand and walked to one of the elevator banks. They rode up several floors and all too quickly he was leading her down one hallway after another, until they finally stopped at the end of one.

She could see into the rectangular room just how crowded it was with every Gannon *but* Fiona, and the low heels of her leather boots suddenly wanted to drag on the tile floor. But Gabe drew her through the opened doorway anyway. Her self-consciousness solidified when all conversation dropped as everyone turned to look at them.

It was Colin, Gabe's father, who broke the awkward lull. He stepped forward and took her hands before dropping a light kiss on her cheek as if it were perfectly natural for him to do so. "It's good of you to come. I know Fiona will be pleased to see you."

"Thank you." Gabe's hand on the small of her back was the only thing keeping her grounded. "I'll be glad when I can see her, too."

Colin moved slightly to one side, looking at his wife, who

was sitting on the foot of the single hospital bed, a magazine open on her lap. "Astrid?"

The woman tossed aside her magazine and looked at Bobbie. "Hello, Bobbie," she greeted, though her eyes were anything but welcoming. "That's short for Roberta, I presume?"

Bobbie kept her smile from dying through sheer grit. "Yes." If she really *were* engaged to Gabe, she'd have been terrified of having the intimidating woman as her mother-in-law.

"Hmm. I suppose Bobbie suits you better." Her tone was smooth, but Bobbie still had the distinct impression that Astrid hadn't meant it as a compliment.

"I think it does," Gabe agreed, and his tone made it clear that it *was.* He picked up Bobbie's cold hand and pressed a kiss to the back of it.

Astrid's lips twisted in a mockery of a smile before she picked up her magazine again.

Bobbie was just relieved not to be under the cool stare of the woman. She nodded a murmured greeting at Gabe's brothers and their wives, who were perched on the only chair the room offered and the wide windowsill. "Where are Todd and Lisette?"

"Stephanie took them down to the cafeteria for a drink," Renée supplied. She gave her a look. "She'll be back."

It was more of a threatened promise than a friendly warning.

Bobbie glanced around the crowded room. Renée was still filing her long fingernails. Diana was busily texting on her BlackBerry. Paul and Liam were leaning against the wall in the corner, talking quietly as if they were anywhere other than a hospital room. Only Colin looked truly concerned for his mother. His suit coat was abandoned, his red tie was loosened and he'd folded his shirtsleeves up his arms.

She decided that she could maybe like Gabe's father after all.

She slid her arm through Gabe's, and looked up at him with a smile. "Why don't we go find them," she suggested.

He looked surprised but then nodded. Before leaving, Bobbie looked back into the room. "Can we get something for anyone?"

Colin just shook his head and did another three-pace circuit. Bobbie figured nobody else would respond—as if it were a crime against the one they figured Gabe *should* be with— and bit back a faint sigh.

"I'd love a coffee," Diana announced before they stepped out the door.

Bobbie looked back, surprised. The other woman had slid her BlackBerry into her case and was watching Bobbie with a vaguely puzzled look. As if she couldn't figure out why Bobbie had made the offer.

"Sugar or cream?" The woman looked as if she hadn't partaken of either pleasure in a decade.

"Artificial sweetener," Diana said. Then she smiled a little. "Thank you."

"Sure." Bobbie glanced around, but Diana's words hadn't managed to break through any significant dam with the others. She and Gabe left the room and she slid her hand into his, feeling his warm fingers weave with hers.

Considering there was nothing permanent—nothing long-term—about her engagement to Gabe, she knew she had no business feeling a spurt of victory at even the smallest sign of acceptance from his family.

No business at all.

Chapter Eight

Despite the doctor's assurance, it was hours before Fiona finally returned to her room. By then, Gabe's brothers and sisters-in-law had departed, as had his mother. Colin remained, though, and Bobbie knew better than to suggest Gabe go home and get some rest.

He had managed to convince Stephanie to leave the children at the hospital with him, however, while she went off to her husband's business dinner.

Bobbie had fully expected another dose of Stephanie's vitriolic attitude, and had been surprised when none had been forthcoming at all. Maybe it was because the children were there, listening, or maybe it was because they were in a hospital. Whatever the reason, she'd been relieved when the other woman had suddenly capitulated and left the kids in Gabe's care.

Unfortunately, that meant that Lisette and Todd had been forced to sit around for hours, too.

And even if they'd badly wanted to see their great-grand-mother, the long wait had definitely been taking its toll on their patience.

When Fiona was delivered in a wheelchair back to her hospital room, only the fact that the children were there kept Bobbie's tears at bay. Her dear friend had never looked so worn. And for the first time, it was almost easy to believe that Fiona had just turned eighty-five.

Once the nurse had gotten Fiona situated with the various wires and tubes tethering her and departed, Fiona let Todd use the buttons to raise the bed more until she was sitting up to her liking.

"Can we do it again?" he asked hopefully, holding the controller.

"It's not a video game, dummy," Lisette scoffed.

Fiona grinned, though her eyes were tired. "I'd rather be playing video games right now," she assured him. "You can play with this darn bed all you want tomorrow if you get to come and see me." She eyed Colin. "Go home and get some rest. You look like *you're* the one ready to have a heart attack."

"Don't joke," he chided, bending over to kiss her cheek. "You gave us a scare. I've been telling you for several years now that it was time you cut back. Those dogs don't need you working yourself to death."

"Don't exaggerate. And it's not the dogs I do it for, as you well know." She patted his cheek and looked at Bobbie and Gabe. Despite her health crisis, there was still a glint in her eyes. "Soooo. Some mischief has been afoot? I suspected there was more going on than repairs over at the carriage house and once I saw you together last night, I knew I was right."

Bobbie felt her cheeks go hot. "Fiona—"

"We can get into all that later," Gabe assured, giving his children a pointed glance.

Fiona rolled her eyes, but she dropped the subject easily enough. "Payroll isn't done. Bobbie, you have a key to the office. Could—

"Mother—" Colin started, but she just waved his protest aside.

"—you go to the office and bring me the checkbook? It's locked in my desk, but you know where the key is. I'll sign the checks. All you have to do is fill in the same amounts for everyone as the last pay period and get them back to the office for Cheryl to hand out before the end of the day tomorrow."

Bobbie stared. She'd pinch-hit any number of tasks at the agency over the years, but never had anything to do with the nine paid employees' compensation.

"Mother," Colin said again, this time with enough steel in his voice that Bobbie had a sudden impression of him in a courtroom. "You do *not* need to be signing those godforsaken paychecks," he said flatly.

But Fiona eyed Colin with just as much steel, proving where he'd come by the trait. "I'm the only signer on the account," she pointed out. "And when I want your opinion, I'll ask for it."

He gave an irritated sigh and turned away from the bedside. "Talk to your grandmother," he told Gabe, who was standing at the foot of the bed. "She listens to *you*."

"Bobbie can sign your name for you," Gabe told her without hesitation. "At least this once. Nobody's going to come charging after anyone for fraud, after all. And I'll get new signature cards from the bank tomorrow so you can get someone else added on to the account."

Fiona crossed her thin arms over the pale-blue hospital gown that she was nearly swimming in. "Fine. Bobbie?"

She lifted her shoulder in a shrug, feeling distinctly uncomfortable. "I'll do whatever you need, Fiona, you know that."

Fiona suddenly smiled benevolently. "Yes, I do know that,

my dear." Then she looked at Todd. "You can push the button to lower the bed now. After all the poking and prodding I've had, I want some sleep, assuming I don't get caught in the web of wires they've got going here." Her gaze went back to the adults as the motorized bed started to lower. "Now, go on and get out of here. I'm told I probably won't kick the bucket tonight, so you can come back and see me tomorrow."

"Mother," Colin chided in a tone that told Bobbie he knew he was fighting for a lost cause, but he leaned over and kissed his mother's cheek again. There was no doubt of his affection for his mother, even if she did exasperate him. He gave Bobbie a smile and clapped his hand over Gabe's shoulder as he left.

"All right. You, too," Fiona looked from Bobbie to Gabe and back again. "The last place Todd and Lisette want to be is hanging out in some musty old hospital."

It was a poor description of the comfortably modern, high-tech institution. "You're not gonna die, are you?" Todd wrinkled his nose. He was still holding the remote control for the bed, his fingers stroking the sides of it.

"Heavens, no. Not today," Fiona assured him. She reached out her arms. "Give this old lady a hug. You, too, Lissi."

Both kids easily bent over their great-grandmother, hugging her as enthusiastically as she hugged them.

Bobbie blinked hard and looked down at the floor. A moment later, Gabe's hand closed around hers.

Startled, she looked up at him. But he wasn't looking at her. He was watching his children hug their great-grandmother with a stark expression on his face.

She knew in that moment that it no longer mattered what her reservations in the beginning had been regarding the wisdom of their little deception. She couldn't stand by and not do something to help him.

Her hand squeezed his and his gaze slowly came around to

her. "It's going to be okay." Her words were nearly inaudible. But she knew he heard.

And when he lifted their linked hands and brushed his lips across her knuckles, she also knew that no matter what their brief future together held, she was never going to be the same.

When she managed to drag her gaze away from him, it was only to find Fiona's attention focused squarely on them. She looked decidedly satisfied and Bobbie felt warmth begin to creep up her throat. She vainly willed it to stop.

The children finally moved aside and Gabe let go of Bobbie's hand then, to get his own hug in. Then it was Bobbie's turn, and she kissed Fiona's gently lined cheek. "Don't scare us like this," she whispered.

Fiona patted her hand. "Don't you waste time fretting about me when you've got much more interesting things to concern yourself with." She glanced past Bobbie and her smile widened. "Like all of *them*."

"I…right." The flush sped up unstoppably and she quickly changed subjects. "Don't worry about the agency, either."

Fiona leaned her white head back against the pillows. "I'm not. Now off with you." She flapped her hands as if she were shooing flies. But there was still a faint smile on her lips, even as she closed her eyes.

Bobbie gathered up her purse and long-dry raincoat and followed the children and Gabe out of the room.

"Can we go back to Bobbie's?" Lisette suggested when Gabe asked what they wanted to do about dinner.

Todd, who'd run ahead of them to punch the elevator's call button, started nodding, too. "We could have pizza and play with the dogs again!"

Bobbie bit back a smile and tried to pretend she wasn't ridiculously touched. "I think Zeus and Archimedes are the real draw." They all stepped into the empty elevator when the doors slid open.

"Bobbie might have other plans for the evening," Gabe said mildly and she suddenly found herself the focus of two sets of very anxious eyes.

"No." She smiled a little shakily. "No other plans at all."

Todd gave his father a "duh" sort of look that amused Bobbie so much she forgot all about that tender shakiness. "What?" She tugged lightly on Todd's ear. "You think there's no way on earth I might have something else to do?"

Todd's cheeks went crimson. Bobbie laughed out loud and caught the boy's face in her hands, giving him a smacking kiss on the forehead. "I'm just teasing you," she assured. "I would like nothing better than for you all to come over. And I'm sure that Zeus and Archimedes will be very happy to see you, too. But maybe we can come up with something a little more nutritious than pizza."

He went from red-cheeked to looking suspicious in a heartbeat. "I don't like spinach," he warned hurriedly. "Or anything else green."

"Todd," Gabe inserted, "you'll eat what's put in front of you. Even green vegetables."

Bobbie bit back another grin as the boy's expression went from suspicious to purely horrified. "What about carrots?" she asked.

Todd gave the matter some consideration. "I guess they're okay."

"Then I think maybe we can manage something." She didn't know what, considering the yawning caverns that masqueraded as her kitchen cupboards, but fortunately, she could call Tommi on the way home for some advice, and nobody would be the wiser. "What about you, Lisette? Anything you don't like?"

The elevator arrived at the ground level and they stepped

off. Lisette tucked her pale hair behind her ear and handed Bobbie her backpack while she put on her jacket. "I don't care what we eat as long as we get to sit on the floor. Mother *never* lets us sit on the floor."

Compared to the former Mrs. Gannon—witchy attitude aside—Bobbie figured she'd more often than not come up short. "Well, if I *had* a kitchen table at all, I can assure you that we'd be sitting at it." She returned the backpack.

"Then I'm glad you don't have one." Todd was matter-of-fact. He trotted ahead of them toward the automatic door and his backpack—camouflage-green in comparison to Lisette's pale-blue—bounced between his shoulders. "It's more fun."

Only because it was a novelty to them, she figured, as they followed Todd outside where it was still raining.

"I'm parked in the north forty," Gabe said. "Wait here while I get the truck. Then I'll drive you to yours." Not waiting for an argument, he set off at an easy jog, his long legs eating up the distance.

She couldn't remember the last time someone worried that she might get wet walking to her car. Had someone—other than her mother—ever worried about that?

She dragged her thoughts together and looked back at the children. "What do you usually do for meals at your dad's house?"

"We go to restaurants mostly, 'cause the only things he can cook are tuna sandwiches or steak on the grill."

Bobbie grinned. "I don't want to alarm you, but my repertoire doesn't include much more than that."

Todd rocked back and forth on his shoes. "Can you make macaroni and cheese?"

She nodded.

"Out of a box?" Lisette gave her an intrigued look.

"Well. Yes. I can make it in the oven, too, though." Tommi had given her a recipe for it that used about four kinds of cheese and took hours to prepare. She'd made it once and promptly decided that if she ever wanted it again, she'd go to her sister's bistro and order it.

"The box kind is what I want," Lisette said with certainty. "I had it once when I was at a sleepover with my friend Ellie Roman." She leaned closer. "We made it ourselves." She whispered it as if it might have been a crime.

"Was it a long time ago?"

She shook her head and tucked her hair behind her ear again. "Before Christmas. But then their cook found out and he got mad and told Ellie's mom he was going to quit if she didn't keep the nuisances out of the kitchen. That's what he calls Ellie and her little sister. The nuisances." She let out a breath. "I never cooked anything before. It was fun. Until we all got in trouble. Louisa—that's *our* housekeeper—says the Romans' cook is a—" more whispering "—lunatic."

Bobbie wasn't certain that she didn't agree. It was also inconceivable to her how the things she considered everyday were not part of Lisette's and Todd's world at all.

She tucked her arm through the girl's. Even at twelve, Gabe's daughter was nearly as tall as she was. "My sister Tommi was cooking in the kitchen before she was Todd's age. Now she owns her own restaurant."

Lisette's eyes rounded. "Cool."

"I've always thought so. Maybe we'll all go there sometime."

"Tonight?" Todd asked just as Gabe pulled his truck up to the curb and pushed open the passenger door from the inside.

"Not tonight. She's closed." Bobbie nudged them forward and they darted across the sidewalk, scrambling up into the back seat of the big truck. She brought up the rear, and once inside, pointed out the location of her car to Gabe.

"Why don't we leave it for now," he suggested. "I'll bring

you by later to get it after we go by the agency to do the checks for Fiona. No point in having us both driving when we'll have to backtrack this way, anyway."

Bobbie was fully aware that it was feeling too much like a cozy family inside his truck, with his long-fingered hand casually resting on the console just a few inches from her arm and his kids squabbling over the video game that Todd had in his backpack. No matter what she'd agreed to help him with, she knew it would be smarter to find some distance. To go to her own car, even if it did mean a little extra driving in the rain.

Which just proved how little she cared about smarts, when she blindly reached for the safety belt to fasten it around her. "Okay, but we'll have to stop at the grocery store to pick up a few things on the way."

"You should have said so. We'll just go out," he said immediately.

"No, Dad!" Lisette poked her head between the seats. "Bobbie's gonna make us macaroni and cheese. Out of a box!"

Gabe looked from his daughter's unusually animated face to Bobbie and felt a dangerous warmth inside him. "Little did I know that cheap mac and cheese could get such a positive reaction."

"Does that mean we don't gotta have carrots?" Todd asked from the rear.

"We'll have carrots, too," Bobbie said, giving Gabe a smile that seemed a little shaky around the edges. "And maybe orange slices. We'll just have a whole orange-colored theme going on in honor of Halloween tomorrow."

Lisette giggled and sat back in her seat. Gabe looked at Bobbie. "You don't have to do all this, you know." The more time they spent together, the more his children accepted her as part of his world, the easier it would be to tell them about the "engagement." And the better it would be in court for him if any questions arose about his and Bobbie's supposedly altar-bound relationship. He knew it. But it was getting damn hard to remember that was his only motivation.

"I know I don't have to." She lifted her finger and he realized that the traffic light had turned green.

He dragged his head out of the gray mist of her eyes and drove out of the parking lot. Rush-hour traffic had abated and it didn't take long to get to Fiona's neighborhood and the grocery store that Bobbie directed him to.

When his kids scrambled out of the truck and raced to the row of shopping baskets lined up outside the entrance, arguing over who would get to push it, Gabe shook his head again. "You'd think they'd never been in a grocery store."

Bobbie looked up at him. "Have they?"

He started to answer, only to realize he didn't know.

And wasn't that a helluva note? Something so ordinary, yet something he'd never done with his own children. And he couldn't be certain, but he doubted that it was something their mother had done with them, since Stephanie had grown up in a house full of servants, and even when she'd married him had expected to keep on a full-time housekeeper. The fact that such a luxury was not in his budget since nearly every dime he'd been making had gone back into expanding Gannon-Morris had been one of the more minor bones of contention between them.

"Relax. It's only a store." Bobbie patted his hand before sliding out of the truck. She flipped the hood of her raincoat over her head and darted after the children.

But Gabe knew it was more than that.

It was one more reminder of the kind of life his children led with their mother and stepfather.

He didn't *want* his kids growing up insulated from such simple, normal things. He'd grown up that way. And if it hadn't been for Fiona's encouragement, he'd have never found his way out of the privileged life that had felt like it was strangling him even before he was out of his private high school.

Bobbie had reached the wet row of shopping carts stacked up outside the store. She pulled one out, propped her foot on the bottom rack, and pushed off, sailing across the empty sidewalk toward the store. Her hood fell off her head and the tails of her jacket swung out behind her as she rode the careening cart.

He heard his kids laugh. Both of them. And beneath that, he could hear the musical sound of Bobbie laughing with them.

He even could feel the corners of his own lips start to turn upward. Addictive, that laugh was.

He let out a low breath, shoved his balled hands in the pockets of his leather jacket. In the right one, his fingertips felt the sharp edges of a flower-shaped hair clip.

He took it out and looked at it. The little jewels on it sparkled beneath the parking lot lights.

He didn't know why he still hadn't given it back to her. Or why he kept carrying it around with him.

He pushed the tiny thing back in his pocket, pushing aside, too, the speculation that wasn't leading him anywhere he ought to be going, and followed them into the store.

In the end, what should have taken only a few minutes to gather up what they needed for dinner took considerably longer. And when they left the store, they were all carrying bags. But when they arrived at Bobbie's place, both Lisette and Todd quickly lost their avid interest in the groceries they'd chosen in favor of Bobbie's dogs. Once Zeus and Archie were out of their kennel and free to play, all four of the youngsters—human and canine—were rolling around on the floor in the living room.

Gabe pulled the last box of macaroni and cheese out of the

reusable fabric bags that Lisette had insisted they purchase instead of using plastic and handed the box to Bobbie where she was loading things into what had been a nearly empty cupboard. "I can't remember the last time I heard Lissi giggle like that."

Bobbie glanced up at him. "Kids and puppies. They're a pretty surefire combination."

"You're the surefire combination," he countered.

Her eyes widened a little and then she blinked, briskly shutting the cupboard door and bending over to the lower one to noisily pull out a large pot that she handed him. "Mind filling that with water? I've gotta find the lid."

He took the pot, and figured there was a hot spot in hell waiting for him, considering the way he couldn't pull his gaze away from the view she made bending over to root through her cupboard. And when she reached an arm in even farther, the back of her short orange sweater rode up a few inches, baring the creamy skin at the small of her back. A sheer stretch of narrow purple with a tiny bow at the center peeked above her blue jeans and even though his kids were giggling from the other room and his grandmother was in the freaking hospital, the only thing he wanted to do right then was to let his fingers do the walking over that bow and beyond.

"Hey, Dad?"

He swallowed an oath, jerking around like he was thirteen and had been caught looking at pictures of naked ladies. "What is it, Lissi?"

His daughter gave him a shy smile. "I'm glad we came here."

Bobbie made a faint sound and straightened, too.

"I'm glad, too, honey," he agreed quietly.

Then Lisette smiled again, a little less shyly, and she pirouetted out of the kitchen. A second later, they could hear her and Todd whispering, followed by peals of laughter.

He swallowed and shoved the pot under the ancient faucet. A moment later, Bobbie set the pot lid on the counter.

"Thanks." Her hands slid over his as she took the filled pot from him to set on the stove. She didn't look at him. "You don't have to stay in here and help, you know." She turned on the burner and plopped the lid on the pot. "It's not like there's much room left in here, anyway." She waved at the dog kennels taking up half the floor area.

In answer, he reached for the bag of carrots. "Got a peeler?"

She looked like she wanted to say something more, but just pressed her soft lips together and pulled open the drawer next to the stove. She rooted through the contents for a moment, then pulled out a vegetable peeler and handed it to him.

But he caught her hand, along with the peeler. "Thanks."

"It's just a vegetable peeler."

His thumb rubbed over her knuckles. "You know that's not what I mean."

Her lashes swept down. "I know." Her voice was low. "But you—we—don't need things to get any more complicated than they already are. Right?" She looked up at him then, giving him a blast of her soft gray eyes.

Eyes that were practically pleading for him not to bring any more hurt into her life.

Yeah, he'd wanted her the day they'd met. When she'd latched her lips onto his and blown every thought of every single thing in his life right out of his mind. And with every day since, that want was becoming even more sharply hewn.

But after that, what did he have to offer a young woman like her? A woman who deserved the whole deal. White roses and rings and picket fences and babies.

Things he'd tried once and had failed at so miserably that he—and those he'd hurt along the way—were still paying the price.

So he made himself nod. Made himself agree. "Right," he said gruffly, and slipped the peeler out of her hand. Then he pulled out a carrot and began peeling the damn thing.

But the only thing he was seeing was the expression on Bobbie's face.

The one that told him she was no more convinced of her words than he was.

Chapter Nine

"I feel like I'm committing some sort of crime," Bobbie murmured later that evening.

Gabe had dropped off the children at their mother's house after their orange-themed dinner, then driven Bobbie to Golden Ability. Now she was sitting behind Fiona's desk, an oversized checkbook flipped open on top of it. Beside her was the salary spreadsheet that she'd somehow managed to find in Fiona's crowded filing cabinets. She consulted it as she carefully wrote out the staff's paychecks.

"You're doing everyone a favor," Gabe reminded her. He was leaning against the doorjamb between Fiona's office and the rest of the administrative space at Golden Ability. "Just sign and stop thinking so much."

She'd be better off if she could stop thinking so much about a lot of things. She clicked the ballpoint pen again and quickly penned Fiona's name.

Only when the first check was completed did she realize she'd been holding her breath.

She let it out and carefully tore out the check, making certain she'd recorded all of the information in the register. "Fiona needs to have all this computerized," she said, moving on to the second paycheck. "It would be a lot easier."

"Tell her that."

"I have." She added the signature, tore it out and enveloped it. Concentrating on this task for Fiona was the only thing keeping her from dwelling on Gabe. "She keeps every other thing around here on the computer. I don't know why she doesn't handle her accounts payable and payroll that way, too, but she just says that she'll leave that task for the next person to run Golden Ability." She shook her head. "As if anyone else could fill her shoes. This place would cease to exist if it weren't for her."

"That would be a shame."

"No kidding." She wrote out a few more checks. "Fiona serves more than a hundred people a year. No fees for them to participate, no charges to be partnered with a service dog. Golden bears the cost for all of it and for an agency this small, that's amazing."

"She ever tell you why she started the agency in the first place?"

Bobbie shook her head and quickly turned her attention back to the checkbook when Gabe suddenly straightened away from his slouch against the jamb and entered the small, crowded office. "I assume what everyone does—that she must have had a heart for it. It's not like she's earned the money that would buy that huge house of hers from the profits."

"She had my grandfather to thank for that." He flipped a narrow, straight-backed chair away from the wall on the other side of the desk and sat down on it, crossing his arms over the top of the back.

"You must have been pretty young when he died."

"About five."

"Do you remember him?"

"Some things. Does Fiona talk about him?"

"Not much." She pressed the end of the pen against her chin for a moment. Her gaze settled on the sinewy lines of Gabe's tanned forearms where he'd rolled up his shirtsleeves, and her fingers tightened around the pen. It was a miserable substitute for the feel of his warm skin.

She looked back down at the checkbook. The cozy office already felt cramped with him there; now she realized it also felt too warm. "I, um, I know she changed everything in her house except his study after he was gone, and never married again. I figured that even after all those years, some losses still remain too deep to talk about."

"He had macular degeneration. He was going blind."

She looked up, and realized she wasn't terribly surprised at the detail. "Which explains why Fiona gained an interest in all this, obviously." She waved her hand around in a loose gesture, then clicked the pen and began tending to business once more. "How did he die?"

"The official story is that he had a heart attack. I learned when I was a teenager, though, that he'd killed himself."

Aghast, she looked up at him. "What?"

"He chose death over a life of blindness."

She pressed her hand to the sudden ache in her chest. "Fiona must have been devastated. And your father, too."

"She never wanted anyone to feel as desperate as my grandfather did about their loss of sight. But the rest of the family just wanted to pretend he'd died of natural causes. To this day, they still maintain that story. And none of the family, including my father, supported Fiona's decision when she started up the agency."

Her lips twisted a little. "Except for you, none of her family seems to support her decision even now, some thirty-odd years later."

"She didn't do what was expected of her. She was supposed to have ladies' teas and sit on the boards of charities. Not run one. She couldn't even count on financial support from the Gannon Law Group. A woman with less resolve would probably have caved to the pressure."

"Is that why you admire her so much? She didn't cave to family demands?"

"She didn't cave, and she backed me when I refused to go to law school."

The more Bobbie knew about him, the more fascinated she became.

And there was danger in that. A danger she wanted to run headlong into.

She realized she was staring at him again and forced herself to look away.

She signed the last of the paychecks and set down the pen again. "You're a successful businessman, though," she managed to say, with a credible degree of calm, considering the way her nerves were dancing around. "I'm sure Colin is proud of you now."

"He might have been if I'd at least become an architect. Instead, I'm a contractor."

"Which is nothing to be sneezed at," she defended.

"It's blue-collar."

"So? Honest work is honest work." Bobbie locked the checkbook back inside the desk drawer and gathered up the sealed envelopes, tapping them neatly into a pile. "And it must suit you. Why else would you spend your entire adulthood making your company a success?"

"Success is relative."

She squared the pile of envelopes on the center of Fiona's ink blotter. It was the only place in the office that was immaculately tidy. The rest of the place was cluttered with books and reports and the odd frippery that Fiona had collected over the last several decades. "I suppose it is."

She pushed back from the desk and scooted out between it and the filing cabinets that lined the wall. She dropped Fiona's desk key back in the ceramic turtle, a handmade gift from the first client that Golden had served all those years ago, and went to the door. "I've never been particularly successful at anything, so I'm hardly qualified to say."

He looked over his shoulder at her, his eyebrow cocked. "You're pretty damn successful, in my opinion."

She tried to squelch the bolt of pleasure his words caused and failed miserably. "All right, I can raise puppies pretty well," she allowed. "But that's certainly not going to get me into the Fairchild hall of fame."

He swung his legs around until he was sitting properly in the chair, facing her. "And what would that take?"

She glanced at the large-faced round clock hanging on the wall. "Don't you want to get going? It's nearly ten o'clock." He was still bearing a heavier load than usual at work because of his injured construction manager, and she couldn't stop thinking how…alone…they were.

He sat forward, forearms on his thighs, his hands loosely linked together. His blue eyes didn't waver from her face. "Turnabout is fair play. You know all the secrets of the Gannon family," he pointed out. "And I'm not feeling particularly hurried."

Which didn't do a thing to calm the butterflies that had been flitting around inside her midsection ever since they'd gone to the grocery store together.

As if they'd been playing house together. Just a quick trip around the grocery with the kids, honey, then back home for dinner and a little homework, consisting solely of creative Halloween costume-planning. For Lisette, they'd come up with a fitting Odette costume made out of a fuzzy white sweater that Bobbie had unintentionally shrunk in the laundry and feathers from a white boa from costumes past. Todd would be a thoroughly hilarious video game character, complete with a French beret that would have probably shocked Georgie—who'd given it to Bobbie as a gift from one of her travels—and a set of fake glasses and mustache.

It didn't matter how good her intentions were to keep things "safe" between her and Gabe: she kept backsliding into the overwhelming allure of him.

And right now, that allure had her wanting to move over to him, to put her hands on those wide shoulders and sink into his lap and...

She dragged her thoughts, kicking and screaming, out of fantasyland. Hadn't they already agreed not to complicate things?

She cleared her throat.

"My mother, Cornelia, raised all of us pretty much on her own once my father died. Frankly, she's the most accomplished, independent, elegant woman on the planet."

"You love her."

"Of course."

The corners of his lips kicked up. "And the other Fairchilds?"

Butterflies danced even more frantically in response to that sexy half smile.

She swallowed and fixed her gaze somewhere over his left ear. But even that seemed fraught with setbacks, because he had exceptionally nice ears.

She honestly couldn't remember ever noticing a man's ears before.

"Well?"

She hoped he couldn't see the flush riding up her neck when he had to prompt her out of her silence. "My eldest sister, Georgie, has a master's in counseling, but works for the Hunt Foundation, basically vetting out worthwhile charities for them to support. She's based here in Seattle but travels all around the world. She's been in Haiti and I think the Sudan is up next, as a matter of fact."

"Hunt Foundation as in your Uncle Harry."

"It's a philanthropic foundation that came out of HuntCom, yes. Alex—that's Harry's third son—runs it."

"I've seen him in the news," he murmured.

"Right. Well, anyway, what can I say about Georgie? She's this tall." Bobbie straightened her arm above her head, waving at an imaginary height. "Long blond hair. Curves in all the right places. *Loves* to tell people what to do." Her lips twisted wryly. "She's always right, too, which is maddening. She's got more brains than I do curls *and* can play the piano and men's hearts with equal ease. There's nothing Georgie can't do."

"Sounds scary."

Bobbie smiled a little. "Intimidating, maybe, but she still has a heart of gold. Then there's Frankie."

Hand still in the air, she bent her elbow a little. "She comes to about here. More blond hair. More curves. She's next in line—we're stair-steps—she's a librarian at the University of Washington and probably the sole reason why most of the male students there like to frequent the place as much as they do. *Not* your stereotypical librarian. But she's still probably memorized every textbook there by now—and understands them."

Her hand dropped a little more, but still hovered above her head. "You've already met Tommi. She put herself through culinary school and even worked in Europe for a while. Opened her own bistro here and I don't have to tell you her wonderful reviews are well-earned, since you've tasted her food for yourself. But if Tommi could, I think she'd feed every hungry person in Seattle. Love through a full tummy. That's Tommi."

She dropped her hand altogether. "Then there's me. The one who usually has dog hair on her clothes, who barely managed to graduate from community college at all. We all got money when we graduated from high school, from Uncle Harry. My sisters used it for their educations and smart things." She shook her head. "Not me."

"Okay, I'll bite."

Her gaze got caught in his.

An entirely different meaning to the words shivered through her.

"I, um—" She blinked and marshaled her too-easily scattered thoughts. "I spent the last of it on Lawrence's campaign, actually." If nothing else could, surely *that* foolishly naive act would take the warmth out of Gabe's eyes.

"You believed in him."

"And he believed I had access to *real* money. Hunt money, remember? All things being relative, my last ten thousand dollars was a pittance compared to that." She plucked her raincoat off the coat tree jammed into the corner of the office.

"That doesn't mean what you did was stupid."

Her fingers crumpled the coat. "It sure felt that way when he dumped me."

"Are you still in love with him?"

If anyone had asked her that even just two weeks earlier, she wasn't sure what she'd have said.

But that was before she'd kissed—then met—Gabriel Gannon.

She moistened her lips and slowly turned to face him. "No."

He studied her for a moment, as if weighing her answer. "Good for you."

She wanted badly to turn the question on him.

Was *he* still in love with his ex-wife? No matter how badly things had ended between them, he'd cared about her enough at one time to marry her. To have children with her.

She'd cheated on him, but that didn't necessarily mean the end of his feelings, even if it had meant the end of the marriage. And Bobbie had seen for herself the tension between Gabe and his ex-wife at Fiona's birthday party. Who was Bobbie to say what emotions were at the base of it?

But the question stayed jammed high in her chest.

Maybe because she was afraid of what his answer would be.

So she stood there, twisting her coat between her hands and after a moment, Gabe pushed to his feet. "It's late. Let's get you back to your car."

She wasn't sure if she felt relieved...or let down.

But she managed a jerky nod and they left the administrative building, stopping only long enough for her to lock up.

The rest of the grounds—classrooms, dining hall and the partially-covered outdoor training areas—were silent with only the safety lights flicking on then off when they walked past. They passed through the front gate, which Bobbie locked behind them. Gabe's truck gleamed wetly where it was parked in the roomy parking lot beneath one of the light poles. She headed toward it, trying not to think anything of his light touch at the small of her back as they crossed the lot.

He'd touched her the same way when they'd danced at Fiona's birthday party, too. Probably just a habit of his. A gentleman and all that.

They reached the truck, and he unlocked the passenger door and helped her up onto the high seat. She gathered her coat around her but he didn't move away and close the door. She looked at him. His eyes were shadowed and mysterious in the light as he looked back.

Her heart suddenly beat a little faster. Her breath suddenly felt a little shorter and then he leaned closer…and reached across her. She heard the safety belt snap into place and realized all he'd done was fasten her in. Like a child.

She swallowed that unpalatable thought as he finally closed the door and walked around the truck to his side and got in.

They drove back to the hospital and her waiting car with only the low sound of music from the radio and the occasional swipe of his windshield wiper blades against the lingering drizzle to break the silence. Finally, by the time the hospital was in sight, that silence felt like corkscrews tightening around her nerves. "I hope your ex-wife won't be upset about the costumes we came up with for Todd and Lisette for school tomorrow."

His thumb slowly tapped the steering wheel. "I don't care if she is or not. At least the kids are happy with what they'll be wearing. They definitely weren't thrilled with the store-bought getups that Steph got them." She felt the glance he slid her way. "Don't worry about it."

"I just don't want to be the cause of any problems."

"I'll worry about Steph. I'm happy the kids have been content to be with *me*. Something else I have to thank you for."

"That's not true."

He gave a rueful laugh. "Yeah, it is. Believe me. So…you didn't say what you'll be dressing up as tomorrow, but I heard Lisette laughing about it when you and she were in your room while Todd and I cleaned up the kitchen."

"Oh, right." She looked out the side window. Did he think it was immature to dress up? "Pippi Longstocking." He was so silent that she finally looked over at him. "Silly, I know, but I've got a few things that'll work for the clothes without much effort, and the only thing I'll have to worry about are getting the braids to stick out from the sides of my head."

"Considering your curly hair, I almost expected a Little Orphan Annie."

"I've already done that one once."

"You dress up every year?"

"Pretty much. Either there's a party to go to, or where I'm working requires it." She gave him a quick look. "Like this year."

"Do you mind? Get tired of it?"

She thought about denying it. But what would be the point. "Not usually. When's the last time you dressed up for Halloween?"

He slowed to turn into the hospital parking lot. "A long time ago."

She plucked at the folds of her coat. "Not since you were a kid, I suppose."

He exhaled. "Steph dragged me to a party when we were dating. I dressed up then. Does that count?"

Suddenly wishing that she hadn't brought up the matter at all, she pulled her purse onto her lap to root through it for her car keys. "Sure. It counts. Um…what—"

"Zorro. And yes, I felt like a damn idiot wearing the mask."

She managed a smile for him. "I'm sure you were very dashing." And his date had probably looked like some svelte bombshell in whatever costume she'd worn. Bobbie knew well enough not to voice *that* question. And fortunately, he'd pulled up behind her parked car, anyway.

Her keys jingled when she pulled them out of her purse before pushing open the door. She waved him back. "Don't get out. I'm fine."

He subsided in his seat. "Thanks again for everything."

"You don't have to thank me." She looked up at the tall hospital building. "It's probably too late to go in and see her again."

His hand slid up her spine, not stopping until he reached the nape of her neck. He squeezed gently. "Probably. Come and see her tomorrow. She'd get a kick out of Pippi."

She didn't know why she suddenly felt tears burning deep behind her eyes, but she did.

Which meant that she needed to get out of his vehicle and into hers before she completely lost her composure. "I'll probably do that. Maybe after my shift at the Bean." She cleared her throat. "Don't forget to take Fiona the signature card from the bank so she can get another signer on her checking account."

"I won't." He could have sounded amused that she'd reminded him of something that he, himself, had suggested in the first place, but he didn't. He just pressed his fingers gently against the back of her neck again, and then his hand moved away. "Do you want me to follow you home?"

"No!" She swallowed and slipped out of the vehicle. "No," she said more normally. "I am a big girl, you know. I can make the drive on my own." And if he followed her back to her place, what were the odds that she'd be able to keep herself from inviting him in?

Not good. Not good at all.

And then he would probably be uncomfortable, and try to let her down without hurting her too-young feelings.

"Drive carefully, then."

She nodded and closed the truck door and went to her own car. She'd just fit the key in the ignition when she realized he'd gotten out of his truck anyway, and was looking down at her through her window.

She rolled it down. "Did I forget something?"

He hunkered beside the car, folding his arms on top of the opened window. "Just for the record, *no*. I'm not still in love with my ex-wife."

Her jaw went loose and her insides suddenly went soft. "I didn't—"

"—ask. I know you didn't." His gaze roved over her face. "Strangely enough, I still wanted you to be clear on that point."

She felt breathless. "Okay."

He nodded once. "Okay." Then he nodded again, straightened enough to lean inside the car, and pressed an achingly slow kiss to her lips. A kiss that said all too clearly that he knew she was definitely not a child. And when he finally pulled away, she could only sit here, dazed and silent. "I'll call you tomorrow."

He thumped his hand on the roof of her car and was moving back to his truck before she could shake herself out of her trance.

Then his truck slowly moved further away in the parking lot and when she saw his brake lights go on and stay on, she realized that he wasn't going anywhere until he was certain that she was safely on her way home.

Fresh warmth spread through her. The kind of warmth that came not just from passion, but from something else entirely.

Something even more dangerous.

Her hand shook as she started up the car and backed out of the parking space. His truck was still sitting there, so she inched past him. Only when she was driving in front of him did he begin driving again, too.

He stayed behind her until their routes home took them in opposite directions. When she heard the staccato toot of his horn as he turned off, she rolled her window down enough to stick her hand out in a little wave.

And then he was gone, his taillights disappearing into the night.

But that warmth stayed inside her all the way home.

Chapter Ten

It took hours for Bobbie to get to sleep that night. And then when she did sleep, it was only to wake up tangled in her sheets and sweating from dreams about Gabe.

Intimate dreams.

The kind of dreams that had you jerking out of your sleep from sheer pleasure, only to realize that it was *just* a dream.

She was due into work at seven-thirty in the morning. And even though she'd set her alarm for the usual ninety minutes earlier, she dragged herself out of bed with an extra hour to spare on top of it.

Staying in bed, trying to sleep, thinking about the man she was engaged-in-name-only to, was just too torturous.

So she took the dogs out for a chilly, dark walk around the block, fixed herself a yogurt and fruit smoothie, and set about transforming herself into some recognizable form of Pippi Longstocking. Once she was finished, she decided she hadn't done too badly.

The yellow dress that she'd sewn red patches all over was really a long T-shirt, but as long as she was careful not to bend over, the hem of it managed to cover the tops of the red and green thigh-high knit stockings that she'd found from a few Christmases ago. And once she'd wrapped enough wiry pipe cleaners around a red headband, she was able to work her two braids onto the wires so they were sticking out oddly from the sides of her head. A dozen freckles painted onto her cheeks with an eyeliner pencil and she was good to go, even if she did earn a few whines from the dogs when she gave them a last pat before leaving the house.

She started to head to the coffee shop, but since she was running early for once, she decided halfway there to face the music with her mother. So she drove to the house that Cornelia had moved them to not long after Bobbie's father had died.

Bobbie had only hazy memories of that first house. It had been much larger and grander. But the place where Cornelia now lived was the place Bobbie had called home and she let herself in without even knocking.

Despite the early hour, her mother was exactly where Bobbie had expected her to be: sitting at the breakfast table with a pot of tea and the morning paper.

She glanced up when Bobbie entered. "Bobbie, dear! What a surprise." She got up to take the jacket that Bobbie was shrugging out of. "Look at you. You've outdone yourself this year. Is everything all right?"

Bobbie let out a breath. "One day I'm going to pop in on you and you're not going to automatically think something is wrong."

Cornelia frowned as she draped the jacket over the back of a chair. "I don't always think that."

"Don't you?" Bobbie bit her lip. "I'm sorry. It's just been a bit of a day." Or two or three.

"It's not even seven o'clock in the morning," Cornelia

chided gently. "And not that I'm averse to seeing you at any time, but this *is* a bit of a surprise." She tugged gently on the end of one of Bobbie's gravity-defying braids. "So...what's wrong?"

Bobbie let out a breath and sat down. "Fiona had a heart attack yesterday."

"Good heavens." Cornelia touched the gold pendant hanging around her neck and sat back down in her chair. She reached across the table to cover Bobbie's fidgeting fingers with her own. "I'm so sorry to hear that. Is she all right?"

"She will be. But that's only part of what I need to tell you." Maybe it was the scare with Fiona or having already gone through a version of this conversation with Tommi, but Bobbie managed to condense matters more than usual when she was faced with telling her always collected mother about her marriage-bound pretense with Gabe.

When she was finished, Cornelia rose again from the breakfast table and moved across the kitchen to look out the window above the sink.

Even at this early hour, her pale-blond hair was pulled back in its usual chignon and she was dressed impeccably in a soft salmon-colored sweater set that perfectly matched her narrow slacks. "Tell me the truth, Bobbie. *Were* you already engaged to this man when Harry told me you were before?"

"No!" Bobbie pushed off her chair and went to stand next to her mother. She could see faint reflections of themselves in the window pane. Cornelia, tall and slender and fair and more beautiful than most women half her age. And Bobbie. Short and rounder in places than she liked, with her dark hair currently confined in ridiculous, wired braids. "If I'd intended to lie to you about any of this, I wouldn't be here now."

Her mother sighed a little and slid her arm around the shoulders of Bobbie's red-and-yellow patchwork dress. "Are you in love with this man?"

"No!"

Cornelia lifted a brow. "Are you certain?"

Bobbie swallowed. "Yes. No. I don't know. I only met him a few weeks ago."

"And look where you are," her mother countered quietly. "You jumped into an engagement with Lawrence after only a month," she reminded. "I don't want to see you hurt again."

"I'll be fine. And *someone* has to help him, Mom. You'd be appalled at his ex-wife's attitude."

"Stephanie Walker. I've met her and her husband, actually, at a HuntCom function last year."

"I told Gabe this was a small city," she muttered.

Cornelia patted her shoulder. "She was perfectly lovely, actually, though maybe a tad uptight about her husband's career. I find it hard to believe that she wouldn't see reason when it comes to the custody of her children."

"She called me *the help* the first time we met."

"Mmm. Unfortunate, of course. And I'm well aware how communications between former spouses can deteriorate beyond all measure. I'm sure you were just too close to the blast range."

Bobbie wasn't sure of any such thing, but she wasn't going to argue the point with her mother. For one thing, she hadn't been shocked right out of her gourd and insisted Bobbie get herself immediately uninvolved—which had been her first reaction when Bobbie had told her she'd planned to marry Lawrence.

"Colin—that's Gabe's father—said he knew you, too."

"Colin Gannon. Of course." Cornelia nodded. She smiled faintly. "Handsome devil. His wife is an interesting woman, as I remember. She didn't strike me as particularly maternal."

"That's one way of putting it. So you're not, um, going to disown me or anything?"

Cornelia tsked. "Where do you get these silly ideas?" She

pressed a kiss to Bobbie's forehead. "I love you, darling. I just want to see you happy."

If it weren't for knowing that her involvement with Gabe was one of necessity rather than emotion, she would have been able to say that she was perfectly happy.

So she just smiled and hoped her mother would take that as answer enough.

Knowing that the morning traffic would be thickening, Bobbie left soon after, and the rest of the day flew by quickly. The shop was busy, and when she wasn't making coffees, she was fielding calls from Cheryl at the agency.

By the time Bobbie got off shift at four, she was feeling exhausted. But the sky was clear for once, so she walked the few doors down to a local floral shop and bought a pot of yellow daisies. They were cheerful-looking enough to give her a fresh shot of energy that carried her back to her car and across town to see Fiona.

Gabe had left a message on her cell phone while she'd been working that he had to run out to Ballard to finish the consultation he hadn't made it to at all the previous day. He'd also visited the bank for his grandmother and the paperwork was still with Fiona. He'd ended the no-nonsense call with "See you later, Pippi."

There was nothing romantic about the message.

No undercurrents in his voice that told her anything other than what his words conveyed.

She'd still listened to it five times in the office at Between the Bean during her lunch break. Doreen, dressed all in pink organza as Glinda the Good Witch, had finally stuck her head around the office door. She'd jabbed her wand—a silver-painted dowel with a foil-wrapped star stuck on the end of it—toward Bobbie. "Just call the man back already if you want to hear his voice so darn bad."

Bobbie had flushed and turned off the phone before finishing her peanut butter sandwich. She hadn't called Gabe, knowing he would be busy enough without having to answer a call from her. What would have been the point of her interrupting him, other than to tell him she couldn't get him out of her head?

But she hadn't erased the message.

And as she drove to the hospital, she couldn't help but wonder if she'd run into him there. She also couldn't help but worry how she would keep up the pretense of their relationship in front of Fiona. The last thing Bobbie wanted to do was cause the woman any sort of stress. If she actually believed that romance had bloomed so quickly between Bobbie and her grandson, telling her that it was all for show was bound to be troubling.

As it happened, though, Bobbie needn't have worried about that.

Gabe wasn't in Fiona's room.

His ex-wife and his children, however, were, and while both Todd and Lisette—dressed in the costumes that they'd come up with at Bobbie's the evening before—seemed genuinely pleased to see Bobbie, their mother most definitely wasn't.

She gave Bobbie a glacial look, but moved aside so that Bobbie could place the large, cheery plant on the windowsill, which was a little crowded, thanks to a big crystal vase overflowing with an amazing orchid bouquet. Bobbie then went to Fiona's side to kiss her cheek. Her dear friend was sitting upright in the bed. "You're getting quite a garden in here," she told her.

Fiona smiled and patted her cheek. "The daisies are lovely, dear. So bright and cheerful. Thank you."

"We brought the orchids," Lisette piped in. She'd completed her swan costume with a white tutu from home and looked quite the young ballerina as she struck poses around the confining room, despite her mother's quiet words to be still.

Bobbie glanced at the impressive floral display sitting next to her very ordinary daisy plant. She glanced at Gabe's ex-wife and tried to remember that her own mother had claimed the woman was perfectly nice. "They're beautiful."

Stephanie smiled back, but the effort could have frozen water. She brushed a languid hand down her perfectly cut, deep-red sheath dress. "The children insisted on visiting their grandmother before getting out of their costumes."

"And I appreciate you bringing them," Fiona put in, giving Todd a wink.

Stephanie looked marginally warmer. "Yes. Well, now they need to be getting home. Ethan will be home this evening and I'm planning a special dinner."

Todd grimaced. "I'd rather be trick-or-treating."

"You're too old for those things," Stephanie told him. "And it's hardly a safe activity, anyway."

Bobbie sank her teeth into her tongue to keep from protesting that. Todd was only ten. Lisette, twelve. And if they had adult supervision while visiting a few of the neighborhood houses, what was the harm?

Todd's shoulders drooped a little.

Even though Bobbie had worried that she would upset the former Mrs. Gannon by helping the children find costumes more to their liking than the plastic ghost-sheet and cowboy vest that their mother had purchased, she was glad now that she had.

At least the kids had been able to enjoy their costumes at school.

She returned their hugs when they offered them, and tried to ignore the frost that returned ten-fold to their mother's expression as she did so. Bobbie was almost giddy with relief when the other woman departed without adding any words to the animosity in her eyes.

When they were alone, Bobbie pulled a bag out of her

oversized purse and handed it to Fiona before scooting one of the side chairs closer to the bed.

"What is this?"

"A few toiletries."

Fiona peered inside, pulling out the comb and the new tube of toothpaste and toothbrush. "Bless you." She took the comb and dragged it through her short hair.

Bobbie smiled, glad that she'd thought to pick up the few simple items. "There's lotion in there, too, and a few magazines. So, how are you feeling today?"

Fiona grimaced at the wires still coming out from beneath her hospital gown, leading to the machines beside the bed. "Like I'm ready to get out of here." She pointed with the comb toward a manila folder sitting on the rolling tray that hovered over the foot of the bed. "Hand me that, will you? It's all of the banking information that Gabriel brought me this morning."

Bobbie handed her the folder, then sat back in the chair again. "Cheryl's called me a half-dozen times today. Everything's going fine at the agency. The graduation for Saturday morning is on course. There's a new crop of pups being turned over from their puppy raisers to the trainers the following Saturday." That particular event was always held in conjunction with a festive picnic. It was one way of honoring and thanking the raisers for being an important part of the process. "I told her to confirm the times and dates with the caterer for the picnic, and to stop worrying so much."

Fiona smiled faintly. She set aside her comb, flipped open the folder and pulled out a sheet of paper that she handed to Bobbie. "Sign by the red X there at the bottom."

Bobbie automatically took the sheet. "For what?"

"To be a signer on the agency's bank accounts."

Bobbie went still. Alarm inflated inside her belly. "Fiona—"

Fiona held up her hand. "Don't bother arguing with me."

"But your son should—"

"—nothing. Colin would sooner close the agency's doors than get involved there."

"Or Gabe—"

"He has enough on his plate." Fiona waved her hand toward the paper. "You're the one I want. So sign."

"But Fiona, I don't even *work* for you. Not that way."

"And I think it's about time we changed that, don't you?"

"And just what would you hire me as? The official check signer? You have no open staff positions. You haven't for two solid years. And why would you? Everyone who comes to work for you at Golden never wants to work for anyone or anywhere else."

"There is a position open. Director."

Bobbie could only stare.

"It's something I've been thinking about for a while," Fiona continued. She flicked a finger against the monitor wires keeping her tethered. "I'm told this was just a warning that I'm supposed to slow down. And frankly, I'd rather do it while I have some control over what happens to my life's work than wait till I'm six feet under and my family gets to sweep everything I've worked for under the rug."

Bobbie leaned forward and closed her hand over Fiona's. "They wouldn't do that."

Without her customary cosmetics, the eyebrows that Fiona raised were pale and faint. "I'm quite certain that they would."

Knowing what she did now about the way Fiona's husband had died, Bobbie couldn't even offer an argument. "They love you, Fiona. If nothing else was apparent at your birthday party, that most certainly was."

Fiona made a face. "Gannons aren't like the Fairchilds,

dear. Love in this family doesn't necessarily mean unquestionable support. I knew it when I married Sean and his mother wore black to our wedding."

"Ouch."

"Indeed. Black might be a fashion choice these days, but back then, it simply wasn't done. It was quite the scandal. She didn't appreciate at all the fact that Sean and I married only a month after we'd met—and she'd had another match already picked out for him. Then I gave Mrs. Gannon—that was my mother-in-law, of course—only one grandchild. Another faux pas, though it was no different than what she had done in her marriage. The only blessing was that she didn't live long enough to see her son die before his time. She would have blamed me for that, too."

"Fiona."

"Don't fret, Bobbie. Gabe told me this morning he let you in on the big family secret."

"I'm so sorry."

"Sean and I had a good life together. It was just too short, and even though I knew he loved me, I also understood the pressure he felt to live up to his family's expectations. When his eyesight was going, he tried to hide it from them all and there was nothing I could do to ease his fears." She shook her head, her faraway expression focusing in again on Bobbie's face. "I like to think Sean's passing wasn't for nothing. It gave me the drive to begin Golden Ability. And now who better to take on the reins than you? You remind me so much of myself when I was young, Bobbie."

"I find that hard to believe. You're always so...focused."

"I found my focus," Fiona countered gently. "Because of circumstances. But you've always been focused when it comes to the agency."

"Sure. Raising puppies!"

"And ensuring that we have other wonderful puppy raisers,

too. And filling in whenever and wherever I needed you. My dear, don't you realize that no matter what else you were doing in your life, you've always stayed committed to your part at Golden Ability? You know the staff. You know what we do and why. Cheryl has worked for me for nearly seven years. She still calls you when I'm unavailable and she has a question about something. I have no doubts that you can do this. And I'm still going to be around to show you the ropes until you're as confident about your own abilities as I am."

A litany of arguments against every point that Fiona was making raced through Bobbie's mind, but she didn't even manage to voice one when Fiona continued.

"And now you're going to marry my grandson." Fiona crossed her arms, looking as satisfied as a cat who'd caught the canary.

Bobbie barely managed not to wince. The litany in her head simply laid down and died. "That's what this is really about. Because I-I'm suddenly engaged to marry Gabe?"

Fiona's head cocked slightly. Her eyes—Bobbie had never noticed before just how similar they were to Gabe's—narrowed slightly. "Actually, one thing has little to do with the other."

Bobbie narrowed her own eyes, trying to read Fiona's. "Are you certain?"

"Have I ever lied to you?"

"No," Bobbie allowed slowly. But there was still a craftiness in Fiona's expression that worried her.

"So sign. At least do that so I don't have to worry about the a/p for a while." She rolled her gaze over to the machines keeping her company. "And so I know if something else does happen, the agency can at least function for a while before Colin gets his hooks in."

"Nothing else is going to happen to you. And I don't want to hear another word from you that it might." She slid the pen off the front of the folder where it was hooked and scratched her signature on the paper. "This does *not* mean anything, Fiona, except that I won't have to forge your name on a few checks. All right?"

Fiona's smile turned angelic. "For now." She pushed a button and the head of her bed lowered a little until she wasn't sitting quite so upright. "Now, tell me how Gabriel proposed. And have you set a date?"

Bobbie nearly choked. They hadn't thought to come up with details like this to support their story. And how could she lie right to Fiona's face? "We, um, we haven't set a date yet."

"I know how everyone loves a June bride, but winter weddings are wonderful, too. And I mean *this* winter," Fiona added. "Not another twelve-plus months down the road."

"What's another twelve-plus months down the road?"

Bobbie looked past Fiona's bed to see Gabe standing in the doorway. Despite the wholly unrestful night she'd had thanks to her dreams about him, relief had her shooting shakily to her feet, and the document she'd just signed slid onto the floor. "Nothing," she said hurriedly before going down onto her knees to fish it out from beneath the metal workings of Fiona's bed.

"Your wedding date," she heard Fiona tell Gabe and when she straightened again, it was to find him standing beside her at the bed, a faint smile on his face as he looked at her.

"Quite an outfit, Pippi," he drawled. His gaze traveled down her torso.

She remembered what she looked like and felt a flush that was surely as bright as the patches sewn roughly onto her T-shirt. She hurriedly dragged the hem back down from where it had ridden dangerously high up her thighs and tucked the paper safely inside the manila folder again. "It's the braids," she said over-brightly. "They make the costume."

His gaze drifted over her thighs once more. "Right." Then he caught her chin with his knuckle and dropped a kiss onto her lips. "The freckles, too."

Bobbie had to forcibly remind herself that the kiss probably was for Fiona's benefit. "I, um, I didn't want to take time to go home and change before I came to see Fiona."

"She brought me the daisies," Fiona inserted.

Gabe glanced at the plant. "Nice." He picked up the folder. "This ready to go back to the bank?"

Fiona nodded and Bobbie skewered Gabe with a look. "I suppose she told you what she wanted."

"Yup." He tapped the folder's edge against the rolling table. "And it makes perfect sense to me."

"I also told her I want her to replace me as director at the agency," Fiona added, "but she's being stubborn. Soften her up for me. I'm sure your persuasive methods are far more enjoyable than my playing on her sympathy."

Bobbie's face felt even hotter. "I'm standing right here, Fiona," she muttered.

Fiona just laughed. "Go on, now. Newly engaged couples shouldn't waste time in boring hospital rooms when there's a date to be set and a wedding to be planned."

"There's nothing boring about *your* hospital room," Bobbie assured feelingly. But she figured exiting as quickly as possible was probably a good idea under the circumstances. She leaned over to give Fiona a careful hug that wouldn't have her T-shirt riding up too high and then followed Gabe out into the hall.

"You might have warned me," she murmured once they'd reached the safe distance of the elevator and were riding down to the main floor.

"About this?" He lifted the folder. "That's Fiona's deal with you. I'm just playing the courier."

"Well, just because my signature is on those papers doesn't

mean I'm going to go along with the rest of her idea." She plucked at a loose thread on one of her patches. "I'd be a disaster." Even contemplating taking Fiona up on her offer had her feeling panicky inside.

"Why?"

"Because!"

He lifted his brows slightly. "Again…why?"

She exhaled noisily. Their acquaintance may have been short, but Gabe should understand her shortcomings by now as well as anyone. "Forget it. Are you taking that thing back to the bank now?"

He glanced at the sturdy black watch around his wrist. "If I can make it before they close." The elevator doors slid open and he settled his hand at the small of her back as she stepped out first.

She pulled in a silent, careful breath and was glad he couldn't see her face. All he'd done was touch her back and she wanted to dissolve.

They turned in the direction of the front entrance and his hand fell away. "Are you heading home now?"

"I don't know if there will be any trick-or-treaters who make it around to the carriage house, but I want to be there just in case." She ruthlessly bit back the suggestion that he join her. "And, um, you?"

"I'm in an apartment. Never had any kids come by before."

"Not even Todd and Lisette, I suppose." She tried to focus on buttoning her jacket rather than the brush of his arm against hers as they neared the doorway, and failed miserably. "Your ex-wife brought them by to see Fiona. They were still there when I got here. They both looked adorable."

The sliding doors opened. "I'm glad at least one of us got to see them."

She looked up at him, then. "Maybe they're still dressed up. You should go by and see."

"Can't. I've got a meeting back at the office at six with a new commercial developer, plus my attorney's been playing phone tag with me all afternoon. I need to find out what he wants. Where are you parked?"

She automatically gestured toward the right, but her mind wasn't on her vehicle. Gabe wouldn't have been able to come by her place even if she'd asked, and the disappointment that swept through her was intense and all the more disturbing as a result. "Well, good luck then, with all of that." She started to step off the curb, but he caught her arm, holding her back from walking in front of an SUV.

She felt the solidness of him standing behind her and after a shaky moment, made herself straighten away from him. "Thanks."

He squeezed her shoulder. "You just need to watch where you're going." Then he tugged lightly on the end of her braid and headed off the curb toward his own truck that she could see parked to the left of the entrance.

She watched his long legs eat up the distance.

He was right.

She did need to watch where she was going. Most particularly where he was concerned, or she was going to end up with her heart hurting in ways that it had never hurt before.

Chapter Eleven

Bobbie waved her hand at the two adults standing behind the trio of children dressed like a band of pirates who'd just scored a handful of candy from her bowl of wrapped sweets. Then she closed the door, leaning back against it for a moment. Zeus and Archimedes were lying on the floor next to her couch. They both had bands over their heads with devil horns sticking up from them, but the lazy thumps of their tails were hardly devilish.

They'd behaved beautifully all evening, not once getting upset or agitated over the surprisingly frequent buzzing of her ancient doorbell or the unfamiliar children who greeted the opening of her door with varying decibels of "Trick or treat!" She tossed them each a small, crunchy dog treat before carrying her empty candy bowl into the kitchen to refill it. The dogs were so well behaved already, she knew that she could turn them over even now to an assistance trainer and they'd do well, even if it was several months earlier than scheduled.

Her doorbell rang again, and she turned back around to answer. Even before she pulled the door open, though, the dogs scrambled to her feet, woofing softly, as they crowded around her.

"Guys," she chided and pointed. "Sit."

They sat, but Archie still whined under his breath.

"Maybe not so ready, after all," she told them, and scratched her fingers over his nose while she pulled open the door, a smile already on her face.

But it wasn't another costumed child, holding up a plastic pumpkin for a treat.

It was Gabe.

And after that first, quick leap of excitement inside her, she realized he looked more harried than she'd ever seen him. His hair looked like he'd been combing it with a garden rake and there were lines around his eyes that hadn't been there when she'd seen him just a few hours earlier.

Her pleasure abruptly turned to worry. "Is Fiona all right?"

His frown was quick. "Yeah."

She let out a relieved breath and pulled the door open more widely. "Come on in. I wasn't expecting to see you."

He stepped into her living room, his hands dropping to the dogs' heads. "Even they get the Halloween treatment, huh?"

She lifted her shoulders, suddenly feeling foolish. "The kids who came by seemed to like it."

"Had some takers after all, then, did you?"

She held up the empty bowl. "Enough to go through the first batch." She headed back to the kitchen again and carried the full bowl back out to the living room. "How'd your meeting go?" She held the bowl out to him in offering.

But he shook his head and she set the bowl on the table by the door.

"I ended up having to reschedule," he said. He paced across the small confines of the living room. Zeus and Archimedes trotted after him. "The custody hearing has been moved up."

"Why?" Alarmed, she sank down onto the arm of the couch. No wonder he looked stressed.

"Because of Ethan's schedule. HuntCom's now sending him to Europe in a few weeks, instead of a few months."

"And just like that—" she snapped her fingers together "—the hearing is rescheduled?"

"Ethan works for HuntCom. What they want has a lot of sway in this area," he reminded her a little grimly.

Bobbie's nerves started to knot, but he said nothing more about her connection to the company. "That doesn't seem very fair," she said after a moment.

Gabe shoved his hand through his hair, and looked at Bobbie's face. The freckles she'd drawn on stood out even more noticeably against her pale cheeks. "*Fair* hasn't exactly been part of the equation so far," he pointed out. Not from his perspective, anyway. "So why would now be any different?"

"What can I do?"

His jaw felt tight. He pulled a jeweler's box out of his jacket pocket and held it out to her. "Wear this."

The fake freckles stood out even more. Her gray gaze finally looked away from his and to the box. She slowly took it from him and thumbed it open. She lowered the box to her lap, the tender nape of her neck exposed below her crazy braids as she looked at the ring.

"My attorney wants you to go to court with me."

She shot him a startled look. "That wasn't part of our agreement."

"I know."

Her throat worked. She slid off her perch on the arm of the couch and onto the cushion properly. An inch of smooth thigh was visible above the edge of her high, striped stockings. "I don't have a good feeling about this, Gabe."

"You won't have to say a word when you're there." He'd grilled his attorney on that point.

"Are you sure?" She looked up at him. "I can't lie outright to a judge."

"I know." She couldn't carry off a lie if it was stuck inside a bucket. It was a wonder that Fiona hadn't already seen through their pretense, despite her health crisis. "I wouldn't ask you to." Short of convincing Bobbie to marry him for real before the court date—something he'd actually found himself considering while he'd been blindly driving around the city after his attorney had delivered the news—he didn't know what else he could do.

A real marriage was not an option. Not even if it meant winning his case.

She rubbed the pad of her thumb over the emerald-cut solitaire diamond. "Is this a real diamond?"

It was the last question he expected. "Yeah." He cleared his throat. "Band is platinum." And picking it out should have been a no-brainer, yet he'd stood in that infernal jewelry store studying one ring after another, trying to imagine which one would please her best.

"It would have been better to get a fake stone," she said after a moment. Her voice was low. "Since everything else about this charade is fake."

"There's nothing fake about how much I need you."

If he weren't so serious, he could have laughed at himself over that one. He'd "needed" her on a visceral level that was probably illegal in some states since she'd jumped into his arms and ordered him to make it look good. If anything, that need had only intensified since then.

She closed her eyes. "You need me because of the children."

He was dying. He needed all his focus on Todd and Lisette. Not on falling for a woman who deserved a lot more than he could offer. He took the jeweler's box out of her unresistant fingers and opened it again. He pulled out the ring.

"Will you wear this?" Everything inside him felt tight, waiting.

She looked up at him, a solemn Pippi Longstocking. Her throat worked in a swallow. And then she slowly lifted her left hand.

He slid the ring into place and her fingers curled. She lowered her hand to her lap and looked at the ring. "It's beautiful," she said huskily. "You, um, you'll tell the kids now?"

"Yes." And they'd be thrilled, which was just another reason to hate himself. "I'll tell them tomorrow."

She nodded and plucked at the hem of her dress then, seeming to realize how much thigh she was revealing. "So when is it? The court date."

"Friday."

"*This* Friday?" She looked alarmed all over again. "Good grief. They really don't give a person much warning, do they?" The doorbell buzzed and she jerked a little. She pushed to her feet and answered the door.

Gabe had to give her credit. His announcement had definitely thrown her for a loop, but she was cheerful and kind when she greeted the two little kids—a boy in a cowboy hat and a girl in fairy wings—and doled out more candy.

But when she shut the door and leaned back against it, her smile disappeared. She looked at him for a long moment, then turned around and opened the door even though the bell hadn't rung, and set the still full container of candy on the step. Then she closed the door, locked it and yanked down the old-fashioned rolling shade that covered the only window facing the front of the carriage house.

His nerves ratcheted up another notch. "You know you've

just guaranteed some enterprising kid a full haul when he takes the entire bowl for himself."

She just shook her head, and reached for one of the red ribbons tied around the end of a braid. "Have a little faith." Blindly working at the ribbon, she straightened away from the door and kicked off her high-heeled, shiny black shoes.

Gabe actually felt his mouth run dry. But all she did was move past him on her way into the kitchen. Zeus and Archimedes trailed after her.

"I suppose you didn't take time to eat dinner, did you?"

Eating had been the last thing on his mind. "No." Feeling some sympathy for the blindly faithful dogs, he followed her, too. "What'd you have in mind?"

"Frozen pizza." She dropped the ribbon on the counter before yanking open her freezer door to pull out a large, flat box that she dumped on the counter, followed by a bottle of wine from her refrigerator that was treated only marginally more gently. "Don't tell Todd or Lisette about the pizza and lack of veggies. They'll never let me forget it." She turned on the oven and yanked open a drawer, rummaging for a moment before unearthing a corkscrew from the jumble. "Here." She handed it to him. "Sorry, but it's just a cheap chardonnay. Otherwise there's still the rest of the orange juice we had with dinner last night."

Only Bobbie could have come up with that color-themed meal and gotten away with it.

His kids had been wholly won over by her.

He cleared his throat. "Wine's fine." Then he picked up the bottle and began peeling away the foil around the cork while watching her jerky motions around the kitchen. She pulled off the dogs' horns and gave them fresh water before starting on putting away the dishes from the night before. "Would you rather I left?"

She looked at him over her shoulder. "I don't know." Then

she shook her head. Her braids stuck out at lopsided right angles from the sides of her head, one with a ribbon, one without. "No."

She didn't sound particularly sure about it, but he decided to take her answer at face value, rather than probe more. Leaving was the last thing he wanted to do.

He twisted the corkscrew into the cork and slowly pulled it out of the wine bottle. "Glasses?"

She opened a cupboard and pulled out two crystal stems. She held them while he poured, and then handed him one. He lifted the glass into the light.

"I know. It's Waterford. Hardly goes with the plastic plates from last night's dinner. But these were a gift and even cheap wine tastes decent when it's in a beautiful glass." She took a drink of her wine and padded back into the living room. "The oven will take a while to heat." She sat down in the leather chair and crossed her legs.

He got another glimpse of smooth, toned thigh.

He threw back a mouthful of wine as if it were a tequila shooter. "How's the floor doing in the bathroom?" He went down the short hallway, feeling an abrupt need to escape.

He still felt her gaze following him. "Perfect. Did you expect it to be otherwise?"

He looked into the bathroom. But instead of surveying the tile job he'd done, his eyes landed on the three sheer bras hanging over the shower curtain rod and the equally sheer panties looped alongside them.

The palms of his hands suddenly itched and he prowled back to the living room. He paced off a triangle in the room, then repeated it. "The ceiling needs painting."

"So do the walls," she pointed out accurately enough. "But I'm perfectly capable of rolling a coat of paint on the walls myself." She sipped her wine, watching him over the delicate crystal.

He knew what was on his mind. *Her.*

But he wished to hell he knew what she was thinking.

"What's your place like? An apartment, you said?"

He was struck by a sense of strangeness. He could almost count on two hands the number of days they'd known one another, but it still felt as if he'd known her much longer. And that, somehow, the prosaic details of his existence had already been covered. "It's just a place to sleep, as far as I'm concerned. There are two extra bedrooms for Todd and Lisette, which have only been actually used once—when Steph left them with me last week." He studied a settling crack in her plaster wall. "I got it just because it was close to the kids. Even the furniture is rented. All my own stuff is still back in Colorado. I built a place there about six years ago."

"And what will you do if you get joint custody?"

"I don't want to uproot them again. I'll buy here. Or build again if I find a lot to my liking."

Her fingertip slowly tapped the rim of her glass, and the ring sparkled in the light. "And if you don't? Will you try again?"

He didn't have to ask her what she meant. "I could keep pulling Steph back into court every time I turned around, even with her out of the country. But what does that end up doing to Todd and Lissi?" He still didn't have a good answer for that. "I don't know. I'll probably go back to Colorado." Following his children to Switzerland wasn't an option. He had too much tied up in Gannon-Morris. If he couldn't keep his kids in the country, the company was the only thing he'd have left.

Her lashes lowered. She sipped a little more wine. "What about your company here?"

"My partner and I can hire a manager, the same as we have for the branch in Texas."

"Wouldn't you miss Fiona?"

"I'd miss a lot of things," he muttered. Not least of which was Bobbie. There was a beep from the kitchen and she started to push out of her chair, but he waved her back. "I'll stick the pizza in."

She subsided and he went into the kitchen. He drank down the rest of his wine in two gulps, unwrapped the pizza and slid it onto the ancient oven rack. He found the directions on the box, studied the front of the oven for a minute and decided there was no timer on it. So he pressed a button on his watch and set the timer there. Then he refilled his glass and took the wine bottle with him back out to the living room.

Zeus and Archimedes had sprawled across the floor, leaving very little space left to pace. Bobbie held up her glass and he topped it off, then set the bottle on top of the crowded bookshelf beside her chair. Then, because he wanted to fill his hands with her, he plucked out one of the photo albums instead and flipped it open.

A younger Bobbie, her curls tumbling from where they were clipped on top of her head, with two full-grown golden retrievers. He flipped the page. More dogs of various ages. More people. A couple of striking blonds he assumed were her sisters that he hadn't yet met. "You should consider Fiona's offer." He closed the album and by some miracle, managed to fit it back into the too-narrow space on the shelf. "You'd be good at it."

She shook her head. "I'm fine where I'm at."

"Serving coffee?"

Her gray eyes narrowed. "Something wrong with that?"

"Not a thing if that was all you aspire to do. Is it?"

She looked away. "I'm not cut out for that sort of work. It's too much of a commitment." Her gaze flicked back to him at the word and he had the feeling they were treading over too-thin boards.

"Are you sure you're not just afraid of failing?"

Her lips twisted. "Well, of course there's that, too." She pushed out of the chair. "I'm going to make a salad to go with the pizza after all. Would you mind letting the dogs out for a few minutes?"

She wanted a little space. It worked for him. He wanted a little space, too.

Maybe then he could remember all the reasons why it was important to keep his hands off her and not complicate the hell out of their arrangement.

He opened the door and called the dogs. They immediately trotted out into the chilly evening, jumping right over the bowl of candy that was not as full as it had been when she'd put it out. But it wasn't empty, either.

She'd told him to have a little faith.

He followed the dogs outside and pulled the door nearly closed behind him before sitting down on the step to watch them. Across the expansive lawn, all signs of Fiona's birthday party had disappeared. Aside from a light that illuminated the back terrace, the house was dark.

He sighed and ran his hand around the back of his neck, then plucked a miniature candy bar out of the bowl and tore off the wrapper. Chocolates and wine and an uncommonly clear night and here he was, sitting on his damn butt while a wholly desirable woman was inside and as off-limits as she'd ever been.

"This is what makes men drink," he told the dogs, toasting them with his wineglass.

Zeus trotted back to him and sniffed at his boots, then moved off again to visit yet another bush. After a few minutes, both dogs returned to sit quietly at the base of the concrete steps. Their tails thumped a few times and he set his wineglass on the step beside him. "How does she let you guys go," he asked, rubbing his hands over their heads.

He heard a soft creak behind him and knew that Bobbie had pulled open the door he hadn't latched. "They're meant for greater things than just being my pets." She stepped out onto the porch and he picked up the wineglass so she had room to sit down beside him.

"Are you going to get cold without a sweater?" He knew plenty of ways to warm her. They marched through his mind with frustrating ease.

But she was shaking her head and wrapped her arms around her bent knees as she looked up at the night sky. "I was getting too warm inside, anyway."

She hadn't been the only one.

"And it's a pretty night," she added.

"Yeah." He looked at her. She'd undone her braids, and her hair—curlier than ever—hung over one shoulder, barely contained in a loop of red ribbon.

His fingers tightened around his wineglass. "You should consider what Fiona's offering you."

He heard her soft sigh. "There's safety in sticking with what I know."

"And there's a lot of life to be experienced when you step outside your comfort zone." He handed her the candy bowl. "You can have faith in complete strangers—kids, yet—not to take more than their share of candy. Have some faith in yourself."

"You've said that before," she murmured.

And he meant it even more now.

She set the bowl behind them. "I'll think about it," she said after a moment.

"Good girl."

"Hmm." She pressed her palms together then looked sideways at him. "Is that how you see me, Gabe? A girl?"

He was suddenly back on those too-thin boards, and they

were creaking ominously under his weight. "You should know the answer to that by now."

"Sometimes I think I do." Despite the small porch light that glowed behind them and the stars that sparkled above, the shadows were still too deep for him to read her eyes. To know whether those gray irises were soft as a fog, or as silvered as liquid metal. She slowly ran her hand along the length of her hair. "Sometimes I don't."

He wanted *his* hand running through her hair.

He looked across to Fiona's house. Creaking boards had become cracking ones. "Bobbie, when I look at you, all I see is a woman." A woman he wanted and should know better than to take.

She drew in a soft breath, leaned back on her hands and stretched out her legs, which seemed impossibly long for someone so petite, until her toes were rubbing in Zeus's ruff. "Even when I'm dressed like this?"

He couldn't have stopped looking back at her if his life depended on it.

He ran his gaze over the goofy yellow dress that clung in all the right spots, down over the smooth skin on her thighs to the edge of her crazy, striped socks that reached well over her knees.

"Even now." He tossed back the rest of his wine. "Especially now."

She drew in a long breath that only succeeded in drawing his attention even more keenly to the taut curves of her breasts beneath the thin fabric. "Gabe—"

His watch suddenly began beeping and they both jerked.

He stifled an oath and shut off the noise. "Pizza should be done."

"Ah. Right." She nodded and gathered her feet beneath her again to stand. She stepped around him, her thigh brushing his shoulder, and went inside.

He exhaled roughly. He didn't need any freaking pizza.

He needed a cold shower. Extremely cold.

He wrapped his hand around the hard iron railing and pulled himself up and followed her inside. The dogs came after him and he closed the door, only to open it right back up again when he realized there was smoke billowing out of the kitchen. He strode into the kitchen and found Bobbie crouched in front of the opened oven, which was clearly the source of the smoke.

"I burned the pizza."

"I'm the one who set the timer."

She closed the oven door, but stayed crouched there, her back toward him. "I'm the one who set the temperature fifty degrees higher than it should have been." She raked her fingers through her hair, got caught on the ribbon tied around it, and yanked out the bright red length, pitching it onto the counter where it slithered off the edge onto the floor. Archimedes sniffed at it, cocked an ear toward Bobbie, who wasn't watching, and looked as if he were going to steal it, only to think better of it when he turned and looked at Zeus. Both dogs wandered back into the living room.

"I can't even bake a damn pizza," she was saying, "and *you* think I can run Fiona's agency?"

He set his wineglass on the counter and went up behind her, sliding his hands beneath her arm. He lifted her to her feet and turned her around to face him. "It's just a pizza."

"It's the story of my life," she countered thickly.

He tipped her face up. The freckles she'd drawn onto her cheeks were smearing beneath a track of tears and he slowly rubbed his thumbs over them. "Then write a new story."

Her shimmering eyes held something he couldn't decipher. "Will you be in it? Or come next week, when your custody hearing is finished, one way or the other, will I be a thing of the past, too?"

He could feel his jaw tightening again. Now that he knew her, could he imagine her absence from his life?

"You don't have to answer that," she said into the silence. She twisted her face away from him and scrubbed her hands down her cheeks. "Pizza is obviously toast. What kind of dressing do you want on your salad?"

He caught her shoulders again and pulled her around to him. "Forget the damn salad." Then he covered her mouth with his.

She made a soft sound that rippled through his blood and he pulled her even closer. Her hands slid around his neck, her mouth opening beneath his. She tasted headier than any wine and he'd never felt more parched with thirst.

He dragged his mouth from hers, hauling in a harsh breath. He wanted her so badly it was a physical ache. "If I don't leave now, I'm not going to leave at all tonight."

She looked up at him, her lips red and swollen from his kiss, bright spots of color burning high in her cheeks. "Would that be so bad?"

He met her gaze. "You tell me."

She drew in a deep breath, the hard peaks of her breasts easily visible through the soft fabric of her dress.

And then she was suddenly reaching for the hem of that dress, drawing it over her head and he had the drowning feeling that he was never going to be the same again.

She held the dress out to the side and released it and it seemed to fall almost in slow motion to the floor, leaving her standing before him wearing nothing but brief black panties, a sheer black bra and those crazy red and green stockings that he was pretty sure were going to give him gray hair if he didn't peel them down her legs and soon.

"Is this enough of an answer for you?"

He couldn't have managed a word just then to save his own life. And he couldn't seem to make himself care, just then, that he'd told himself again and again why things would be better—safer—if they didn't head down this road.

So he nodded and reached for her, and was damned to realize his own hands were trembling while she seemed not to hesitate at all as she slid her palm against his, threaded her fingers through his, and turned to lead him out of the kitchen, down the short hall and into her bedroom, which was lit only by the whisper of moonlight shining through the window opposite her bed.

She let go of his hand then, and even in the dim light he could see the silvery gleam of her wide eyes as she slowly slid off her bra, her hands hesitating shyly over the high thrust of her bare breasts for a moment. Then she lowered her palms to the edge of the panties that skimmed the tight curve of her hips. She slowly drew them off and started to reach for the thigh-high socks.

He caught her wrists, though, and silently shook his head. Her lips parted a little. Her fingers curled softly and subsided at her sides.

He wanted to race his hands over every inch of her silky, pale skin, but he controlled the impulse to rush, to hurry, to plunder and take quickly before she realized what she was doing, before she changed her mind, before she turned him away.

So he grazed his fingers over the slender slope of her shoulder, and watched the way her eyes fluttered and the pulse at the base of her long throat visibly beat.

He traced the lines of her collarbone, skimmed along the outer curves of her breasts and watched the pale crests turn crimson and pearl even more tightly. He felt the narrowness of her waist, the inviting flare of her hips and the shadowy down at the juncture of her thighs that promised more heaven than he was sure he could survive.

He nudged her back a step, then two. Her legs met the bed and she slowly sat. He trailed his fingers down her legs, behind her knees and he heard her catch her breath a little, a hitching sound that snuck down inside him and twisted his nerves into a fresh, torturous knot. Then he found the elastic edge of the high stocking and slowly rolled it down her smooth, shapely leg.

She drew in another shuddering breath and moistened her lips, leaving behind a distracting glisten. He tugged the knit stocking off her leg and dropped it on the floor. Before he could reach for the other, she silently leaned back on the mattress, her elbows supporting her, and lifted her leg, delicately placing her toes in the center of his chest. Her gaze met his. Challenging. Waiting. Inviting.

He wondered then just who was leading this dance, and decided it didn't matter. He slowly rolled down the second stocking and tossed it aside, then bent her knee as he leaned over her and took her lips.

He felt her murmur his name through his kiss, and her hands tugged at his shirt, then his belt. He raised up long enough to get rid of the annoying clothes separating them, and then he was covering her again and her arms were holding him, and before he could think another coherent thought, she was guiding him into her and she felt so tight, so wet, so *home,* that he could have cried like a baby.

He sucked in oxygen through his clenched teeth, pressed his forehead against hers and tried to remember that she was a petite woman and he was not a small man. He didn't want to crush her. But she was wrapping her strong legs around him, her hips urging his on and on and on. And then her mouth was burning over his shoulder, his neck, as he felt fine ripples start exploding at the ends of his nerves.

"Don't stop," she begged when she reached his ear. "Please, Gabe, don't ever stop."

And then she cried out and he felt her convulsing around him and all he wanted to do, all he *could* do, was follow her again.

Right into the fire.

Chapter Twelve

Bobbie heard the buzzing of her doorbell and rolled over, feeling an unfamiliar, delicious ache in her muscles, and peeled her eyes open to peer at the clock.

It was just after seven in the morning.

She inhaled, and slowly ran her hand over the rumpled pillow beside her own, unable to stop a silly smile.

Gabe had stayed the entire night and she hadn't even had to ask him to.

Reality was *so* much better than dreams.

She let out a contented sigh, then held the pillow to her face, imagining the scent of him there. She could hear the rattling of her water pipes. Gabe was taking a shower.

The doorbell buzzed again like an angry bee, distracting her from her delight, and she sighed, tossing aside the pillow as she rolled out of bed. The morning air was cold and she shivered hard, grabbing up the blue crocheted afghan off the floor to wrap around herself as she headed out of the bedroom.

Her footsteps hesitated as she passed the bathroom door. It was ajar and steam was rolling around the doorframe.

Shivers danced through her, the memories of Gabe's love-making exquisitely fresh.

Would he like it if she joined him in the shower?

The doorbell buzzed again and, sighing, she put aside the temptation. She went to the front door and yanked it open, not sure who she expected to be on the other side, but it certainly wasn't the woman standing there on the step.

Gabe's ex-wife.

Stephanie's hair was pinned back from her face and a trench coat that Bobbie recognized as seriously expensive was wrapped around her slender form. Even in the thin light from the early sun, the other woman's gaze ran over Bobbie, from her thoroughly mussed hair to her bare shoulders to her equally bare toes peeping out from beneath the blanket.

"I guess I can tell why it took you so long to answer the door." Stephanie's voice was as cold as the morning air.

It was all Bobbie could do not to cringe. It was bad enough that she could feel her skin flushing as if she'd been caught doing something terrible.

Gabe was a free man. She was a free woman.

And as far as his ex-wife was concerned, they were even engaged to be married.

Why shouldn't they spend the night together?

Wishing like fury that she'd bothered to put on something more substantial than a ridiculous afghan, she kept her shoulders straight with an effort. "What can I do for you, Stephanie? Are the children all right?"

The other woman's lips thinned. "They're fine, except that Todd left his book in Gabe's truck the other day and he needs it for his reading class this morning. Believe me, I have no desire to track his father down like this." Her gaze raked down Bobbie again, her distaste more than obvious. "When

I couldn't reach him at his apartment or his office, I figured he'd be here with *you*."

Bobbie knew that, no matter how objectionable the other woman was, the polite thing would have been to invite her inside. But she just couldn't make herself do it. "I'll get his truck keys," she said and turned away from the door.

The shower was still running when she went back to the bedroom, and she found Gabe's keys in the pocket of his jeans, which were still lying in a heap on the floor.

She pushed her bare feet into fuzzy slippers and exchanged the afghan for an oversized Mariners sweatshirt that nearly reached her knees. Then she went outside.

Stephanie was waiting by Gabe's truck, her arms crossed and her toe tapping, as if Bobbie had deliberately taken her time. Ignoring her, Bobbie unlocked the truck and peered into the back where, sure enough, a thin reading book had slipped beneath the seat. She pulled it out and handed it to Stephanie. "I'm sorry we didn't notice it earlier."

Stephanie didn't acknowledge the words as she took the book and turned toward her own car—a sleek BMW that Bobbie figured was worth more than she'd earned in the last five years combined. "Tell Gabe not to forget our appointment with Toddy's counselor this afternoon."

Bobbie highly doubted that Gabe would have forgotten it, but she had no desire to antagonize the other woman. "I will."

Stephanie pulled open her car door and tossed the book inside. But instead of getting in, she looked back at Bobbie. "He'll break your heart, too, you know."

At first, Bobbie wasn't certain she'd even heard right. She stared at the other woman across the uneven pathway and it slowly dawned on her that Stephanie's rigid posture wasn't entirely formed by disapproval.

Bobbie also knew that she was afraid of that very thing—a

broken heart—just as she knew it was already too late to prevent it.

It had been from the night she'd walked up Fiona's terrace
for the birthday party and Gabe had held out his hand toward
her.

But she took a few steps toward the other woman. "I think
he's worth taking the chance."

"Hmm." The other woman looked over at Gabe's truck.
"I suppose you're young enough that you can afford to think
that way." She looked back at Bobbie. "I'm not anymore. All
I have are my husband and my children. Ethan has given me
everything that Gabriel wouldn't, and he wants me at his
side when he goes to Switzerland, and I want to be with him.
Gabe's intent on destroying that. You do realize that, don't
you?"

Bobbie took another step closer. She could feel the hard
edge of the stone paver beneath her soft slippers, and let the
solidness of it ground her. "Gabe's not trying to destroy anything. He's just trying to hold onto his children."

"By taking them away from me."

"By *sharing* them with you!" She lifted her hands. "Stephanie, all he wants is to be their father, but how can he do that
when they're halfway around the world?"

"How can I be their mother if they're halfway around the
world from me?" Stephanie's voice rose. "He hates me. He'll
turn them against me."

Bobbie shook her head. There'd been an edge of something painful and hurting in Stephanie's voice that made the
other woman seem suddenly far more human than before.
"He wouldn't do that," she said quietly.

"He's hauled us all back into court," Stephanie clipped.

"Because you've given him no other choice! That doesn't
mean he's trying to turn your children against you."

Stephanie gave a cool smile that was nevertheless tinged

with something sad. "I've known Gabe for more than twenty years. How long have *you* known him?"

Bobbie didn't answer that.

How could she?

Because the truth of the matter was, she had only known Gabe a matter of weeks. And even if every cell inside her said to trust him, what had her judgment in the past ever shown her other than that her judgment was all too fallible? "All I know is that the two of you managed to create two really wonderful children. Maybe the only thing you have in common anymore is your love for them, but that's still a lot of love that Todd and Lisette deserve to know. It just seems to me that there ought to be a way for you to work things out."

Stephanie just shook her head and tsked, the cool, superior tone right back in place as if it had never been displaced. "Young *and* naive. I wonder how much your connection to Harrison Hunt will shield you when those qualities wear off?" Then she slid into the car and closed the door with a soft, final click.

A moment later, she was backing out of the long drive, and then driving off.

Bobbie exhaled.

So Stephanie knew about Harry, too.

Was that why she'd kept her claws mostly sheathed? Did even she think Bobbie held some sway when it came to Harry and HuntCom?

She slowly turned and went back inside, taking the now-empty candy bowl that was still sitting on the step with her. She called the dogs out of their kennel where they'd been sleeping and let them outside for a few minutes. When they came back in, she had a pot of coffee brewed and the shower had finally stopped.

She filled a sturdy white mug with coffee and carried it to the bathroom door, knocking softly. "Coffee?"

The door opened and Gabe stood there in front of the mirror, one of her plain white towels wrapped around his hips.
"Thanks." His smile was slow and easy as he took the mug
from her and she felt her insides melting all over again. "You
need a new showerhead."

Bobbie blocked out Stephanie's words that wanted to twine
through her mind. There would be time enough to worry about
Gabe's ex-wife. Right now, she knew her time with Gabe was
slowly ticking down to the custody hearing and she was feeling very protective of that time. If it meant wringing every
moment with him that she could out of it, then that's what
she would do.

So she leaned her shoulder against the doorjamb and put a
faint smile on her face. "Know any available handymen who
might want to help me out?"

His eyes narrowed as he sipped the hot brew, then he set
the mug on the little shelf near her sink. "I think I might." He
looped his fingers into the collar of her sweatshirt and reeled
her toward him. "Did the shower wake you up?" He nudged
her head back to kiss her chin. Her nose.

Her breath shortened. "No." Her hands settled on his wide
chest, her fingers pressing into his warm, damp skin. She
would never get tired of the feel of him, even if she had fifty
years to enjoy it. "We had a visitor," she murmured as his lips
settled over hers.

He tasted like her minty toothpaste, only far, far more
delicious.

"Hmm?" His hand cradled the back of her neck as he drew
her even closer. His other hand dragged at the long sweatshirt
until she felt his palm meet the skin of her thigh. Then her
hip.

His fingers trailed teasingly around to the small of her
back, drifting lower over her rear.

"Stephanie," she managed before she could forget how to speak altogether.

His hand paused.

"Todd forgot a book in your truck the other night." She wriggled a little, until her backside felt the delightful warmth of his palm again. "He needed it for today." She trailed her hands down his torso, loving the feel of his tight muscles bunching beneath her touch. He might be forty-one, but he had the tightest abs she'd ever seen. And since she'd once done a brief stint as a receptionist at a fitness center, she'd seen plenty.

She grazed her knuckles over the edge of the towel, very much aware of the hard length of him barely contained beneath it.

"She say anything else?"

Bobbie pressed her lips against his collarbone. Tasted the moisture still clinging there. "Nothing important."

His hands slid beneath her rear and he lifted her onto the chilly edge of the sink, then he stepped between her knees and she forgot all about the cool porcelain beneath her. "I don't want her upsetting you."

"She didn't." *Not exactly.* Bobbie ran the sole of her foot along the back of his leg. "What time do you have to be at the office?"

He smiled faintly. His damp hair was tumbling over his forehead and his blue eyes gleamed. His hands delved beneath the sweatshirt again, setting off ripples of delight as his fingers skimmed over her waist, walked along her ribs, and then slowly curved around her breasts. His thumbs brushed circles over her nipples until they felt positively frenzied. "I'm the boss, remember?"

"Thank goodness." Her voice had gone breathless. She tugged at the towel and it slid off his narrow hips. She leaned forward to nibble at his chin, then his lips. Her fingers grazed over the length of him, loving the feel of that velvet-covered steel. "I want you, Gabriel Gannon, like I've never wanted anyone."

His chest expanded against her. "Good. I'd have to kill the other guy if you did." His hands moved suddenly, and she had to let go of him when he pulled the sweatshirt over her head. He tugged it off her arms and pitched it aside, then filled his hands with her breasts. "Perfect," he murmured, and bent low enough to capture one peak between his lips.

Sensation streaked from her breast straight to her core and her head fell back until it hit the mirror behind her. She ran her hands over his shoulders, then slid them along his corded neck. She sank her fingers into his hair and tried not to cry out when his teeth gently grazed her, followed by the slick heat of his tongue.

"I know something else that's perfect," she managed. Her thighs slid along his, her ankles looping behind his back. Even hunched over her the way he was, she could feel the nudge of him against the very heart of her, demanding and very hard where all she felt was wet and wanting.

She lifted her hips toward him, flushing at her blatant invitation, but was too far gone to care. Besides, she had been pretty blatant the night before, and that hadn't exactly sent him running for the hills. "You inside of me," she finished throatily.

His lashes lifted and his gaze met hers above the achingly tight nipple he was tormenting with his tongue. The faint lines at the corners of his eyes crinkled a little and then his lips were burning along the valley between her breasts, then upward, ever upward until he'd straightened again and his mouth was hovering a hairsbreadth away from hers. "I wouldn't want to disappoint a lady," he murmured.

His hands curved around her hips, slid beneath her bottom and lifted her onto him.

She cried out, nearly convulsing right then and there as he sank into her so deeply, so completely, that she felt consumed.

She hauled in a shaking breath. Then another. "No disappointment here," she finally managed and felt her heart fall open even more when he gave a short bark of a laugh.

"What am I going to do with you, Bobbie?"

Love me. The words rang insistently inside of her head. But she just smiled into his eyes. "Make love to me."

The corners of his lips kicked up in that faint smile that never failed to make her breathless. "That—" his hands cradled her rear "—I can definitely do."

Then she felt the pulse of him reach to the very center of her and her head fell forward, her forehead resting in the heated crook of his neck.

She could hear the charging beat of his heart, could feel the raggedness of his breathing and she twined her arms around his shoulders, clinging for dear life when he lifted her a few inches, then lowered her again. His name was in her breath. His body was in her very cells. And then he was moving again, and she shuddered, clinging ever tighter as he carried her out of the bathroom, down the hall and back to her bedroom.

A thin band of sunlight from the window was creeping across her tumbled mattress as he slowly lowered her to the bed, never parting from her. And when she drew his weight down over her, she cried out again.

His mouth found hers, his fingers twined with hers as he slowly, devastatingly thrust into her, until every molecule of her soul felt ready to explode. She gasped and he raised himself up on his hands, the cords in his arms and his shoulders standing out. The pleasure was almost more than she could bear.

And then, when his gaze finally lowered, hers followed

and she realized the band of sunlight was slowly widening. It flowed across her breasts, her abdomen, and the heat inside her flamed even brighter as if Gabe directed the golden light himself, stoking it wider, brighter, until that ray of light was cutting over their bodies where they were joined as closely as two could ever be.

Her breath caught as she hung at the edge of an exquisite precipice, dangling there at his mercy, at his pleasure. And then he whispered her name, roughly, half broken, and just like that, she slid so smoothly, so perfectly, over the edge, her head falling back, her eyes closing as she tumbled into bliss, giving him everything that she was.

And she knew that in this moment, at least, he was giving her everything in return.

"This was the best start to a day that I've had...ever." Gabe's arm was wrapped around her waist, holding her on the running board of his truck. The sun was steadily climbing above the horizon. "Is it bad etiquette to say thanks?"

She grinned. "I'd be hurt if you didn't."

His eyes crinkled. "Then thank you." He punctuated it with a kiss. "Thank you." Another kiss. "And thank you." Another. Then he slapped her playfully on the rear. "Now go inside before I blow off the entire day."

"I have to go brew coffee for people, anyway."

"As long as you don't accompany it with the kind of service you treated me to."

"I have some standards, you know. I don't—" she waved her hand in the air "—you know, with just any customer."

"Glad to hear it," he drawled. "Or men across Seattle would be dropping like flies from heart attacks. It's a wonder *I* survived."

She rolled her eyes. "Being the ancient soul that you are and all that, I suppose. I guess for an old guy, you did fairly well." She hopped down onto the ground, her slippers barely cushioning her feet against the hard ground, and gave him a mischievous smile.

"I'll give you old," he warned, smiling slightly.

A shiver danced down her spine. "I do hope so."

He muttered an oath and shook his head. "Go inside, woman, before I forget we both have jobs to get to."

Smiling, she turned on her heel and sauntered back to the house, giving him one last look over her shoulder and nearly laughing with delight to find that he was still watching her.

After she went inside and closed the door, she heard his engine start, and then the crunch of his tires rolling over the drive.

Still smiling, she raced into the kitchen to feed the dogs. She picked up her Pippi costume, which was still lying in the center of the kitchen floor, and felt herself flush all over again at her own wholly unfamiliar boldness. She went into the bathroom and took a quick shower, raked some smoothing lotion through her wet curls before pulling them back in a ponytail and put on clean clothes.

Only when she was ready to step outside her door did she suddenly slow down.

She held out her hand and the diamond ring on her finger winked up at her.

The narrow, nearly white band fit perfectly.

She curled her trembling fingers into a knot and the diamond caught the light again, sending prisms dancing across her living room. She exhaled shakily.

If only the intent behind the ring was as real as the diamond itself.

The day passed quickly once Bobbie reached the Bean, with plenty of customers to be served, while in between she and Doreen switched the Halloween decorations—ghosts and spiders—for cornucopias and stuffed turkeys wearing pilgrim hats. She tried not to keep checking her cell phone to see if Gabe called, but it was hard.

On her lunch hour, she raced over to Tommi's bistro for a panini. Her sister was too slammed with customers to do more than lift her head when Bobbie poked hers into the kitchen for a second, and maybe that was just as well, because she wasn't sure what she'd have said to Tommi about Gabe if she'd had enough time to talk. Knowing her sister, Tommi would probably have known right off that something major had occurred.

And Bobbie wasn't ready to have the fragile connection she had with Gabe picked apart. There'd be time enough for that after his custody hearing.

So she took her panini with her back to the Bean, and even by the time she finished her shift, her phone was still stubbornly silent. No calls from Gabe.

She drove to the hospital to visit Fiona, but she was dozing over a magazine, so Bobbie quietly sat down in the side chair and stared out the window, watching the clouds slowly drift in the sky, moving in, then out of the sunbeams.

She sighed. She'd never again be able to look at a shaft of sunlight and not think of Gabriel...

"That's a pretty heavy sounding sigh."

She looked over at Fiona. "I hope I didn't wake you."

Fiona waved her hand. "All I've been doing is sleeping," she dismissed. She yawned as she closed her magazine and set it aside. "So is that a Gabriel sigh or something else?"

"Fiona—"

"Oh, relax, dear. I'm not going to grill you about your engagement." She exhaled tiredly and leaned her head back against her pillow. "I know it's not real."

Bobbie blinked. "But...how? Did Gabe tell you?"

"Heavens, no. All I have to do is look at your face whenever the subject comes up."

Guilt swamped her. "We never intended to lie to you, Fiona."

"I figured that, too. And I suspect you never intended to fall in love with my grandson, either."

Bobbie stared. "I—"

"—can't even deny it," Fiona inserted gently. "Just because I'm an old woman doesn't mean I've forgotten what it feels like to be swept off my feet with love for a man when you least expect it."

"It's not going to get me anywhere," she said huskily.

"Hmm. Maybe. Maybe not. Gabe felt responsible for the breakup of his marriage, even if it was Stephanie who did the cheating. I'd dearly love to think he'd get over that self-blame and find the sort of future he deserves. I suppose this little pretense of yours is to aid his cause where Todd and Lisette are concerned?"

"Yes."

"Well. I'm certainly not going to judge you on that score. I don't want my great-grandchildren spending the next several years in another country, either. Gabe's been fighting this issue for longer than he should have had to."

"His children are what matters most to him."

"And what matters most to you, Bobbie?"

Bobbie's lips parted, but words felt elusive. "Not letting everyone around me down."

"What about letting yourself down?" Fiona leaned forward until she could catch Bobbie's hand in her own. "I've known you for more than ten years, Bobbie, and you have more enthusiasm and passion for life than anyone else I know. You're far harder on yourself than you need to be. So what if you've had a lot of different jobs. It's given you experience in a dozen different ways. And so what if you don't have a PhD or a graduate degree? With all of these dogs you've raised, you've touched the world in ways that most people can never imagine. I hate seeing fear of making a misstep hold you back. Life isn't always about the perfect decision at the perfect time in the perfect place. It's also about all the missteps we make in between."

Bobbie realized her cheeks were damp. She swiped her hand over them. "Golden Ability is too important."

"It's too important to be left to someone who doesn't care about it as much as you do." Fiona squeezed her hand. "I *know* you can do this, Bobbie."

Bobbie inhaled. Could she?

Everyone around her seemed to think she could.

If she wanted more out of life, didn't she have to take the step?

"Okay," she said on an exhale, and then had to sit there, still, while the world seemed to spin around her just a little.

"Good girl," Fiona said.

Another rush of tears burned suddenly behind her eyes, but she blinked them back. "I hope none of us end up regretting this," she muttered.

"Well, I know I won't," Fiona assured. "Now. Go find me some lime Jell-O, would you? It's the only thing around here that is remotely appetizing, since they won't let me have cheeseburgers and fries."

Bobbie laughed brokenly. She leaned over her friend and hugged her tightly. "I love you, Fiona."

Fiona's hand patted her back. "And I love you. Now stop worrying so much. Everything will work out. Even Gabe."

Bobbie straightened and slid her fingers beneath her eyelashes again. She badly wanted to believe Fiona, but not even she could guarantee her grandson's heart.

So Bobbie went and tracked down the lime gelatin— three little cups of it—and left them with Fiona, along with a promise to come back the next day to start working on the process of becoming the director of Golden Ability. Then she went home to Zeus and Archimedes, who'd been patiently waiting to be let out.

The light on her message machine was blinking and she jabbed it, fully expecting to hear Gabe's voice at last, but even there she was disappointed.

"Bobbie, this is Martin Paredes. We met at a HuntCom picnic this summer and it's taken me this long to track down a way to contact you." He laughed. "Anyway, I've got two tickets for the Seahawks this weekend, and I remember you had an interest in football, so I thought you might—"

Frustrated, Bobbie hit the *delete* button while he was still talking. It was the only message on the machine.

She exhaled and told herself there was no reason why she had to wait for Gabe to call *her,* but old habits died hard. And one thing Cornelia hadn't raised her daughters to do was chase down a man. Even if he had given her the most incredible night—and morning—of her life.

So she took the dogs for a walk that was long enough to work some of the pent-up energy out of them, fed and watered them, and heated herself a can of soup before sitting down in front of the oven to try to scrape up the mess left by the charcoal briquette that had once been a frozen pizza.

"In my next life, I'm going to have an oven that's self-cleaning," she told the dogs after she'd scraped blackened cheese off the bottom of the oven for so long that her wrist ached and her ears hurt from the screeching sound of metal against metal.

"Take the job that Fiona's offering you and you could afford to buy a decent oven in *this* life."

She dropped her metal spatula and spun around on the floor. The brilliance that suddenly filled her chest at the sight of Gabe standing there was almost scary. "Well, I guess we'll find out, since I told her this afternoon I'd take it."

"You did?" He smiled widely. "That's great!"

She lifted her shoulders, feeling strangely self-conscious. "I'm going to give it my best shot, anyway." It was all that she could do. "I, um, I didn't hear you come in."

"Obviously." He dropped a paper bag from a local fast-food joint on the counter and crouched down to rub the dogs, who looked like they were ready to go into delirious fits of pleasure as a result.

She knew how they felt.

"I knocked *and* rang the bell."

"Sorry." She folded her arms around her knees, afraid that if she didn't contain them, she'd crawl over to him to get his hand on *her* instead of the dogs. "How'd the meeting with Todd's counselor go?"

"Same as always." His smile died and his voice went short. "But since Steph figures she'll be taking them both out of Brandlebury within the next few weeks, that's even more reason not to move him to a different math class."

Forget her intentions. She let go of her knees and instead walked over to him. She ran her fingers through his hair, and settled her palm alongside his jaw. "That's not going to happen."

"Glad one of us thinks that." He took a deep breath and slid his arms around her waist until she was pressed closely against him. She could feel the weariness in him when his head lowered onto her shoulder. "I told the kids we were engaged. Lissi wanted to know if she can be a bridesmaid and Todd warned me that he wasn't going to wear any suit."

Her throat went tight and her eyes burned. If only it could all be true. She stroked her hand through the heavy silk of his dark hair and pressed her lips softly to his temple. "Everything's going to be okay, Gabriel."

But even as she said the words, she couldn't help wondering *how*.

Chapter Thirteen

"Bobbie, this is my attorney, Ray Chilton."

Bobbie managed a nervous smile and shook Gabe's lawyer's hand. "Pleased to meet you."

They were standing outside the courtroom, waiting to go inside where Stephanie, her husband and the children were already seated. The middle-aged man peered so closely through his bifocals at Bobbie that she couldn't help worry that she'd worn the completely wrong thing to a child custody hearing.

"You're younger than I expected," he finally said.

Bobbie felt herself flush, but she managed a smile anyway. "Sorry." She might have been able to take Tommi's advice that her new slate-gray skirt suit was the epitome of conservative and responsible-looking, but she couldn't add on years that she didn't possess.

"Don't let her age fool you," Gabe inserted. "She's the new director of Golden Ability."

"Oh?" Ray cast another look at her as if he were mentally adding that fact to her qualifications as Gabe's fiancée and prospective stepmother to the children he was there to fight over. "Interesting."

Bobbie kept her smile in place. It wasn't easy, though. She still could barely believe that she'd accepted the position that Fiona had offered, not even after having spent most of the previous day with her at the hospital, taking a virtual crash course in running a non-profit.

For now, the plan was for her to begin at the administrative offices on Monday. Fiona was supposed to be released from the hospital by then, and she would spend an hour at the agency with Bobbie each afternoon.

The idea still took some getting used to, though Bobbie had to admit it wasn't as terrifying as she'd expected it to be. And her sisters and mother had been positively thrilled when she'd called to tell them the news. They'd each even claimed that they weren't surprised by the turn of events at all.

The court clerk stuck her head out into the hall, catching their attention. "We're ready," she chirped brightly.

Bobbie suddenly felt a wave of nausea. She brushed her hands down the front of her suit and reminded herself that she was there for appearances only. Gabe grabbed her hand, though, as they entered a courtroom that was hardly larger than her own living room.

She took a seat in the row of seats behind Gabe, and folded her hands in her lap, trying to smile naturally at Lisette and Todd, who were sitting pale-faced and fidgeting behind their mother alongside a tall, good-looking man that Bobbie assumed was their stepfather, Ethan.

She knew the children had already spoken privately with Judge Gainer in his chambers before the hearing had begun, and could only imagine how hard that had been for them.

Were children supposed to have to choose one parent over another?

She inhaled and looked forward again as the judge—a short, gray-haired man—entered the courtroom and took his seat behind a wide desk. Her fingers nervously twisted the diamond ring on her finger while the court clerk read off their purpose there, and then it was a matter of sitting silently while Stephanie's lawyer recounted all the reasons why Stephanie and Ethan should be allowed to retain full custody of the minor children, Todd and Lisette.

After a while even the judge started to look bored, or at least that was Bobbie's hopeful impression.

And then it was Gabe's turn, and she held her breath, watching him approach the stand—which in this case, was simply a hard-backed chair sitting next to the judge's desk. Like Ethan, he was wearing a charcoal-gray suit, and in that moment, he looked much more like his name should be on the masthead of the Gannon Law Group rather than a man who usually wore a hard-hat and work boots, with a roll of building plans resting over his shoulder.

Across the courtroom, his gaze met Bobbie's for a moment, and then he was looking back at his lawyer as Ray started speaking.

She twisted her hands more tightly in her lap until the diamond was cutting an impression into her palm and she forcibly relaxed them. She didn't know how Gabe could manage to look so calm and controlled when she knew beneath that smooth surface he was even more wound up than she was.

"Your honor, Mr. Gannon has proved his dedication to his children," Ray was saying. "He's relocated here to Seattle at some professional cost to his company, Gannon-Morris—"

"Excuse me," Stephanie's lawyer interrupted. "Gannon-Morris *expanded* by Mr. Gannon's relocation here. Their profits are higher than ever. We have copies of Gannon-Morris Limited's financials if—"

The judge waved impatiently. "No, thank you. Continue, Mr. Chilton."

Ray smoothed down his tie and continued pacing in front of the judge's desk. "My client has adjusted his entire life to allow for more time with his children. His standing in the community is well-known; his character references that you've already reviewed are impeccable. There's no reason to believe he's unfit for joint custody with Mrs. Walker."

Stephanie's lawyer rose again. "What about his fabricated engagement to marry Bobbie Fairchild for the sole purpose of making himself look less like the man-about-town and more like a more suitable parent?"

Bobbie went still, her eyes meeting Gabe's again. His expression didn't change one iota. "There's nothing fabricated about it," he said evenly.

The other lawyer leaned over while Stephanie whispered in his ear. Then he straightened again. "You met Ms. Fairchild only a few weeks ago, isn't that right?"

"Your Honor—" Ray started to protest, but the judge lifted his hand.

He was suddenly looking far more interested and he leaned on his arm, directing his attention toward Gabe where he sat beside the desk. "Mr. Gannon?"

"Yes, I met Bobbie a few weeks ago. She rents my grandmother's carriage house and I was doing some repairs there."

Bobbie couldn't help holding her breath, though she knew there was simply no way any of these people here besides Gabe and herself could know just exactly how that first meeting had gone.

"Must have been love at first sight, then," Stephanie's attorney drawled mockingly.

Other than a slightly lifted eyebrow, Gabe didn't respond to the goad.

"My client doesn't make a habit of casual relationships," Ray stated.

"Or serious ones," they all heard Stephanie mutter.

"Control your client, Mr. Hayward," the judge said calmly.

"Sorry, Your Honor," Stephanie's lawyer quickly apologized.

The gray-haired judge's lips twisted a little. He looked back at Gabe. "When do you plan to marry this woman?"

Bobbie held her breath again.

"We haven't set a date," Gabe said, which was true. "My grandmother recently had a heart attack and is still in the hospital. Naturally, that takes precedence at the moment over wedding planning."

"And your fiancée understands," Mr. Hayward said, again sounding mocking.

"Bobbie's the most understanding woman I know," Gabe returned. His gaze met hers across the courtroom.

The judge tapped his pen against his desk for a moment. Then he straightened in his chair again. "I see no reason why Mr. Gannon's engagement should adversely affect my decision here today. In fact, both Todd and Lisette had positive things to say about her."

"Notwithstanding the judgment of *children*," Mr. Hayward said, "since Ms. Fairchild is going to be the stepmother of my client's children—and therefore involved to some extent in their caretaking—perhaps we should hear from *her*."

"Your Honor, Ms. Fairchild's character isn't in question right now," Ray interjected.

"Perhaps it should be," Hayward suggested silkily.

Bobbie wanted to sink through the floor when the judge

cast her a speculative look. "Presumably, you *are* the fiancée in question?"

She nodded.

He gestured her forward. "Come up here, then."

"Your Honor, this is highly irregular."

"And it's my courtroom, Ray," the judge reminded Gabe's lawyer testily, "so I'd like both you and Luke there to shut up and sit down and I'll ask the questions that I figure need answering, if that's all right with you?"

Both lawyers abruptly sat.

"Come up here, Miss…Fairchild, is it?" The judge glanced at his clerk, who nodded.

Certain that everyone would be able to see her knees knocking together below the modest hem of her skirt, Bobbie went forward. The clerk popped up from her chair, looking annoyingly cheerful and perky, and swore her in.

"Have a seat," the judge invited. "Mr. Gannon, you can step down."

Gabe rose and Bobbie met his gaze as she moved around him to take the chair he'd just vacated.

"It's okay," he murmured.

Which meant what, exactly?

That he knew she was going to blow everything for him?

She swallowed the knot in her throat and sat down, staring mutely at the judge.

"That's a nice ring," he offered.

Startled, she looked down at the diamond solitaire. "Thank you." Her fingers curled. "I—I think so, too." That, at least, was the God's honest truth.

He smiled a little. "Family court is a nerve-wracking place to be most times."

She shot Gabe a quick glance. He was sitting beside his lawyer, his blue gaze steady on her face. "I imagine so. I've never been in a courtroom before at all."

"Most people would consider that fortunate." The judge tapped his pen again. "Tell me about yourself."

"Um—"

"Your age, your profession. That sort of thing."

Her shoulders relaxed a little. "Twenty-seven. And I've just accepted the position of director at Golden Ability. It's a canine assistance agency here in Seattle."

He nodded. "I've heard of it."

And how glad she was to say that, rather than that she was a lowly clerk at Between the Bean. Not that she was ashamed of her time working at the coffee shop, but even she knew "clerk" didn't exactly smack of responsibility and capableness the way "director" did.

"I'm also a puppy raiser for the agency," she added. "Which essentially means that I foster pups that eventually go on to become assistance dogs of one type or another. I've done that for about ten years."

The judge was nodding. "Pretty steady work, sounds like. And you've lived in Seattle for a while, then?"

"Born and raised."

"Prior marriages or children?"

She shook her head. "No."

"Excuse me, Your Honor." Stephanie's lawyer rose again. "But our understanding is that Ms. Fairchild *was* previously engaged."

Bobbie realized if she could just keep her focus on Gabe's face, she didn't feel quite so nervous. "That's true," she allowed. She flicked a glance at the judge. "I was briefly engaged to Lawrence McKay."

"The councilmember? What happened?"

She felt a flush working up her throat. "We realized we weren't right for each other." She moistened her lips, waiting for some reminder at any second of the public nature of that particular event. But, thankfully, none came. "He's since married someone else and I'm sure they're much better suited," she added.

"I had a broken engagement myself, before I met my wife," the judge said, casting a censorious look toward Stephanie's table that had the lawyer subsiding in his seat once again. "A broken engagement usually has fewer consequences than a broken marriage. I ought to know," he added with obvious irony. Then he tapped his pen a few more times. "What do you think of your fiancé's children?"

Bobbie relaxed a little more. "They're wonderful, of course. Bright and imaginative and well-mannered."

"Would you be able to provide discipline if it were necessary if they weren't so well-mannered after all, or do you think a stepparent's position shouldn't extend into that area?"

"I'm afraid I don't know how to answer that." She twisted the ring on her finger. "Todd and Lisette have a mother who loves them. I certainly have no expectations of replacing her. But that doesn't mean I couldn't love Todd and Lisette as well." She knew that she already did. She swallowed again, searching carefully for a truthful answer. "If there was some situation where I had to assert my authority, I like to believe that I could."

"And as far as you're concerned, your engagement is not—as Mr. Hayward has implied—manufactured simply to help Mr. Gannon's case here today?"

Gabe's nerves tightened to a screaming pitch.

He looked across at Bobbie, whose gray eyes were so wide they dominated her pale, heart-shaped face.

He leaned toward his attorney. "Stop this now," he whispered harshly.

Ray shook his head. "I can't."

Gabe looked at Bobbie again and wished to hell and back again that he'd never dragged her into this.

She was in agony.

Everyone there could see it.

Then her gaze dropped to her lap. She moistened her lips, then looked to her side at the judge. "I'm wearing this diamond ring for only one reason," she said in a low voice that was nevertheless perfectly audible. Perfectly clear. "Because I'm in love with Gabriel Gannon."

The room was so silent he could hear his heart pounding in his ears.

She had always said she wouldn't lie for him in court.

And he knew, in that moment, that she hadn't.

A pain knotted inside his chest as he willed her to lift her head, to lift her gaze back to him.

But now, she wouldn't look at him at all.

"That's not exactly an answer to Your Honor's question." Stephanie's lawyer was the first one to speak into the hushed silence that followed Bobbie's husky admission.

Gabe saw Bobbie's lashes flutter as she looked back down at her hands.

He pushed to his feet. "It's answer enough," he said gruffly. "She's not here to be picked apart just because my ex-wife is still mad that I wasn't the kind of husband she wanted."

Bobbie's lashes flew up, her gray eyes startled.

"Counselors, it seems to me that neither one of you can control your clients very well," the judge commented. He leaned toward Bobbie. "You can step down now, Ms. Fairchild. I know what I need to know."

She nodded jerkily and rose from the chair and headed toward Gabe. "I'm sorry," she whispered thickly.

"I suppose you're going to make sure that HuntCom takes this out on Ethan, now," Stephanie accused curtly. "What a perfect little fiancée Gabe picked. If the court doesn't rule his way, he can have you ruin my husband's career. Either way, he wins."

The judge huffed, clearly irritated, and picked up his gavel. He slammed it once, hard, on his desk. "Enough!"

Bobbie just shook her head, looking at the other woman. "There's no winning here! And you don't know Gabe as well as you claim if you think he'd stoop to that level. Since you don't know me at all, I suppose I can't blame you for thinking I'd be a party to it." She looked at Ethan. "But *you* work for HuntCom. And *you* should know they don't operate that way either." Then her gaze skimmed over Gabe as she looked back at the judge. "I'm sorry for speaking out of turn."

He grimaced. "Everyone else has." Then he smacked his gavel again. "Everyone out except Mr. Gannon and Mrs. Walker and their legal representatives."

"Come on, kids." Ethan rose and began scooting Todd and Lisette out of the courtroom.

Gabe saw Bobbie's teeth sink into her lip, and then she, too, was heading toward the door, believing what she'd feared.

That she'd ruined things for him.

He couldn't let her go. Not like this.

He went to follow her.

"Where are you going?" Ray clamped his hand on his shoulder but Gabe shrugged him off.

"I have to talk to her."

"If you walk out now, you're just going to piss of Judge Gainer even more. Is that what you want?"

Gabe looked from his lawyer to the judge, and finally landed on his ex-wife. "You know this is wrong, Steph. I'm sorry I hurt you. That I wasn't the husband you needed. If you still need to punish me by taking my kids away yet again— even though you now have with Ethan everything you ever used to want—then I guess you've got to do what you have to." His throat felt tight. "But I won't ever stop fighting for them. They're the only things you and I did right together. And I wish to God that you could see that we could still do one more thing right together, by raising them jointly." He looked from Stephanie's stone-faced expression back to the judge. "Right now my future is walking out that door, and if I let her go, this time I'll have nobody to blame but myself."

Bobbie's heels rang on the tiled corridor outside the courtroom. All she could think of was escape.

"You're right about HuntCom."

She nearly skidded to a stop when Ethan suddenly spoke. He was the only one who'd maintained his silence inside the courtroom, and now he was looking more than a little pained as he stroked his hand over Lisette's head. "Everyone who works there does so on their own merit, and that's all that's ever mattered. I've tried to tell Steph that, but she just can't see reason when it comes to Gabe."

Bobbie lifted her hands, feeling futility in every breath she drew. "I'm sorry."

"Bobbie?" Lisette was giving her a worried look. "Is that judge really going to say we don't get to see Daddy anymore?"

"That's not what this is about, honey," Ethan assured her softly.

Bobbie pressed her lips together for a moment. "Ethan's right," she finally managed. She looked at Todd, too. "You'll always be able to see your dad. He'll make certain of it, even if you do move back to Switzerland." Which, thanks to her miserable performance for the judge, was surely a foregone conclusion.

She pressed a kiss to Lisette's forehead, then to Todd's, who ducked his chin shyly. "He loves you two more than anything, you see? And your dad won't let anything stand between him and the ones he loves." And then, because she didn't think she could hold back her tears a second longer, she straightened.

And found Gabe standing there.

She inhaled sharply. "You're supposed to be in the court-room."

"The judge ordered a recess." His hands were balled in his pockets and his blue eyes were stark. "You didn't lie."

A tear burned its way from the corner of her eye. "I…I told you I wouldn't."

"You couldn't. Even if you wanted to."

Bobbie was vaguely aware of Ethan silently moving Lisette and Todd further down the empty corridor. "I wanted to," she whispered.

"To keep me from knowing that you loved me?"

A fresh ache crept through her. "No." She twisted her arms around her waist, trying to still her quaking. She jerked her chin toward the courtroom door. "To make them believe we were real."

"They believe it," he said quietly.

"But I didn't tell them that."

"You didn't have to." He pulled his hands out of his pockets and slowly closed the distance between them. And when he lifted his hands to stroke his fingers down her face, she realized they were trembling just as badly as she was. "All you needed to do was be you." His jaw cocked to one side for a moment, then centered again. "I knew all along that you were someone remarkable. I just didn't let myself face how much you meant to me until you were walking out of the courtroom and I was suddenly afraid that you would keep on walking. God knows I've given you reason."

Bobbie's vision blurred. Her heart leapt into her throat. She tried to speak, but the only thing that came out was a garbled, "Gabe."

His thumbs slowly trailed along her jaw. "I'm sorry you ever had to answer the judge like that, that I put you in a posi-tion where you had to justify anything about yourself."

"You didn't know," she managed thickly.

"I should have. But whatever happens in that courtroom, I can deal with it, as long as I know I haven't lost you." His eyes stared fiercely into hers as if he were trying to see all the way to her soul. "Have I? Lost you?"

She covered his hands with her own. Drew them away from her face to slowly press a kiss to his palms. And then she looked up at him again, and this time it was she who was seeing through to his soul.

It was right there, open and bare and just as uncertain of being loved as she'd ever felt herself.

Her shaking calmed.

Her heart steadied.

She stepped closer until their hands were caught between them. Caught between her heart and his. "You haven't lost me."

"Are you sure? You deserve more than a guy like me, Bobbie. You deserve everything."

His uncertainty melted her. "Then I deserve *you*." She went on her toes, pressing her lips to his. "And I'm more certain of that than I've ever been of anything in my life," she whispered.

His hands slipped away from hers, but only to draw her against him in a fierce embrace. "I love you, Bobbie Fairchild." His voice was low and thick. "And I didn't think I'd ever love anyone again."

She twined her arms around his neck, her heart so full it could have burst out of her chest. "I love you, too." And then she drew in a shaking breath. Let it out in an even shakier sough. "When I told you to make it look good, I never expected this."

He laughed then, and slowly set her back onto her feet. "Once upon a time, there was a kiss," he murmured.

His gaze roved over her face, full and warmer than any burst of sunlight could ever be. He reached into the inside pocket of his lapel. "And the lucky guy caught a princess." He held out his hand, and a tiny, jeweled hair clip sat on his palm.

Bobbie's chest tightened. "I was wearing them the night of Fiona's birthday party."

"It almost feels like a lifetime ago." He slowly lifted one of her curls and pinned it back with the clip.

Fresh tears fell, but Bobbie didn't care. She stared up into his face. "The lifetime is ahead of us," she whispered.

"A brand-new story?" He lifted her hand, kissing the finger that wore his ring. "One with a white dress and a wedding ring to match this?"

She caught her breath. Then nodded. "Yes. And we'll be together in every chapter."

And when he smiled, so slow and so easy, and drew her into his arms once more, she knew deep in her heart that this time, they'd write their happy ending.

They'd write it together.

Epilogue

"You've got someone here to see you, Bobbie."

Bobbie glanced up from the budget she was studying to see Fiona's—no, *her*—secretary standing there. "Who is it?"

But Cheryl just lifted her shoulders and disappeared from the doorway of Bobbie's office.

Bobbie glanced at her watch, then her appointment book. She didn't think she had anything scheduled, but then she'd only been running Golden Ability for two weeks, and she was still nervous about missing something important. But her calendar was clear and Fiona had already put in her daily allotment of time with Bobbie. Less than an hour, actually, because she'd insisted that Bobbie was doing fine, and she had a new yoga instructor she was working with…a fine young man named Juan.

Fiona was clearly throwing herself into her retirement with as much enthusiasm as she did everything else.

Bobbie left the budget on her desk. She'd already managed

to find several thousand extra dollars by transferring it from one cost area to another, but she was perfectly happy not to look at numbers for a few minutes.

She worked her way out of the office that had grown even more crowded since Fiona's abrupt retirement, smoothing her hands down the sides of her deep-red sweater dress, and walked out into the administrative area.

The sight of Gabe still made her heart skitter crazily around in her chest, and she grinned, quickly crossing to him. "This is a nice surprise." She caught his hands in hers and reached up for his kiss. "I wasn't expecting you. Aren't you supposed to be working?"

"Boss's perks, remember?" His eyes crinkled. "I brought you something." He held up a slender box and she laughed and took the box from him.

"You're spoiling me."

"That's a fiancé's prerogative, isn't it?"

She just shook her head again, and flipped open the box. Inside, was a delicate silver bracelet with three shining daisies dangling from it. "Another one?"

"For some reason, I feel a need to fill your life with flowers." He took the bracelet from her and fastened it around her wrist. "Besides. It matches the necklace."

She couldn't seem to stop smiling. She touched her finger to the diamond pendant that hung around her neck. It, too, was in the shape of a daisy. "And the earrings." She shook her head a little and she felt the dangling earrings dancing in her ears. She looked at the bracelet. "It's beautiful. Thank you." Then she laughed a little. "Little did Georgie know what she was starting when she gave me those hair clips."

Gabe was still grinning. "I have something else for you."

She huffed a little. "Gabe! I have a necklace, a bracelet and earrings. What else is there left?"

"This." He reached into the pocket of his battered suede overcoat, and pulled out a thick sheaf of folded papers. He handed it to her.

"What is it?"

"Read."

Her hands were suddenly shaking. She unfolded the papers. The top was a handwritten letter on fine parchment paper. Bobbie skimmed through the sloping writing. "It's from Stephanie."

"She's agreed to send the kids back before Thanksgiving." His voice went gruff. "And to let them stay until the summer. The rest of the stuff there is a modified visitation agreement, giving me physical custody of Todd and Lissi for the rest of the school year."

Bobbie gasped, pressing her hand to her mouth. She set the papers aside before she dropped them. "I...I can't believe it. When Judge Gainer postponed his ruling and she and Ethan took the children to Switzerland, I was afraid she'd never let them come back here again." It had been the only thing to mar the perfection of the last two weeks. The parting had been agonizing. But she and Gabe had spoken to—and seen, thanks to the wondrous invention of the webcam—both kids every single day since. It wasn't the same as being with them, but it made the situation a little more bearable. "Why'd she change her mind?"

"I told Ray to withdraw my petition."

Shocked, Bobbie sank down onto the edge of an empty desk. "*When?* Why didn't you tell me?"

"Last week. And I didn't tell you because I didn't want you thinking that I'd given up."

Bobbie made a soft sound. It never failed to undo her to realize that for all of his secure confidence, Gabe had his fears, too. "I'd never think that." She touched his hand. "You wouldn't."

His hand turned over, his fingers closing around hers. "I told Ray to let Stephanie know that I wasn't going to keep yanking the kids into our battle. I love them enough to leave them with her, if that was the best thing for them."

Bobbie lifted her eyebrows. "But you've never thought that was the best thing for them."

He grimaced. "Maybe not. But even I had to start facing the fact that, for all her faults, Stephanie does love them." He tugged at the ends of her hair, which she'd tied into a ponytail. "A very smart woman opened my eyes to that fact."

Bobbie smiled faintly. "I'm still surprised." She picked up the letter again, then let out another laugh. "Stunned, really."

"I guess once I stopped pushing, she could afford to start giving a little."

"So it would appear. Personally, I think Ethan might have softened her up."

"Ethan?"

"Well, he's not a stupid man, or he wouldn't be working for Uncle Harry's company, would he?"

His eyes suddenly narrowed. "You didn't—"

She shook her head. "Of course not. But I can't help it if he's wanted to know everything about the man I intend to marry. Harry's very protective sometimes."

"And what'd you tell him?"

"That he can judge you for himself when we see him over Christmas."

"That's all?"

"That's all," she assured softly. "But I'll warn you that he's taking credit for our getting together. Seems to think that if he'd never asked me to show Tim Boering around Seattle, you and I would never have met."

"Fiona would have made sure we did," he said, looking amused.

Then he shook his head and laughed a little.

"So Steph really *did* change her own mind."

"Evidently." Bobbie looped her fingers around the lapels of his thick jacket and tugged him closer. "So the kids will be here before Thanksgiving? That gives us about a week and a half."

"To do what?"

"Find a decent place to live. The carriage house is too small for all of us. It's too small even for the two of us." Though they'd been managing remarkably well since he'd been spending nearly every night with her there. "And your apartment is not exactly homey." In fact, she'd been appalled when she'd finally seen it. Which was why they were always at the carriage house. Even her hand-me-down furnishings were more welcoming than his nearly sterile place.

"Are you suggesting we move in together?" His hands linked behind her back. "I'm almost shocked." His lips tilted wickedly.

She laughed. "I seriously doubt that."

"Okay. We'll find a bigger place to rent until we decide on something more permanent. Maybe we'll find some land and I'll *build* us a home. Satisfied?"

She nodded. A home with Gabe? What more could she want? "Extremely."

"And in the meantime, since the kids will be back soon… how fast can you put a wedding together once they are?"

Bobbie looked at him quickly. "You want to get married right away?"

"A marriage *is* usually the end result of an engagement," he reminded her.

She smiled slowly, then turned around, only then realizing that nearly everyone in the office had been watching them avidly. "Cheryl, I'll be leaving now for the day, if anyone calls."

Her secretary looked surprised, then an indulgent smile crossed her lips. "Sure thing."

Bobbie turned back to Gabe, grinning. "Boss's prerogative," she whispered. Then she hopped off the desk, ducked into her office to grab her jacket and purse and raced back to the love of her life. "Come on." She pulled him out of the building and into the uncommonly sunny afternoon.

Gabe followed, his laughter low and deep. "Where are we going now?"

"To start the rest of our lives, of course."

He caught her around the waist and delight swept through her just as easily as he swept her right off of her feet. Sunlight shined across his face, turning his eyes even bluer. "That started the day we met."

She wrapped her arms around his neck.

Oh, how she did love this man.

"All right," she conceded. "Then we're going to go see Mom and call my sisters." She smiled mischievously. "Because if anyone can organize a wedding in a matter of weeks, it's the Fairchild women."

"Maybe we should take a quick detour along the way." He brushed his mouth against hers. "Because I'm feeling suddenly desperate for just one Fairchild woman in particular."

How easily he could have her blood rippling through her veins. "Maybe a quick detour. But then off to my mother's."

He nodded, looking amused and obedient and wholly sexy all at the same time. He set her back on her feet. "You think all of you can pull a wedding together before the end of the year and not be disappointed?"

Bobbie tangled her fingers with his. "Nothing about marrying you will ever be a disappointment," she promised quietly. And then she smiled brilliantly. "And yes. I'm sure that we can."

And they did.

* * * * *

Silhouette®

COMING NEXT MONTH

Available November 30, 2010

SPECIAL EDITION

#2083 A THUNDER CANYON CHRISTMAS
RaeAnne Thayne
Montana Mavericks: Thunder Canyon Cowboys

#2084 UNWRAPPING THE PLAYBOY
Marie Ferrarella
Matchmaking Mamas

#2085 THE BACHELOR'S CHRISTMAS BRIDE
Victoria Pade
Northbridge Nuptials

#2086 ONCE UPON A CHRISTMAS EVE
Christine Flynn
The Hunt for Cinderella

#2087 TWINS UNDER HIS TREE
Karen Rose Smith
The Baby Experts

#2088 THE CHRISTMAS PROPOSITION
Cindy Kirk
Rx for Love

REQUEST YOUR FREE BOOKS!

2 FREE NOVELS PLUS 2 FREE GIFTS!

SPECIAL EDITION

Life, Love and Family!

YES! Please send me 2 FREE Silhouette® Special Edition® novels and my 2 FREE gifts (gifts are worth about $10). After receiving them, if I don't wish to receive any more books, I can return the shipping statement marked "cancel." If I don't cancel, I will receive 6 brand-new novels every month and be billed just $4.24 per book in the U.S. or $4.99 per book in Canada. That's a saving of 15% off the cover price! It's quite a bargain! Shipping and handling is just 50¢ per book.* I understand that accepting the 2 free books and gifts places me under no obligation to buy anything. I can always return a shipment and cancel at any time. Even if I never buy another book from Silhouette, the two free books and gifts are mine to keep forever.

235/335 SDN E5RG

Name	(PLEASE PRINT)	
Address		Apt. #
City	State/Prov.	Zip/Postal Code

Signature (if under 18, a parent or guardian must sign)

Mail to the **Silhouette Reader Service:**
IN U.S.A.: P.O. Box 1867, Buffalo, NY 14240-1867
IN CANADA: P.O. Box 609, Fort Erie, Ontario L2A 5X3

Not valid for current subscribers to Silhouette Special Edition books.

Want to try two free books from another line?
Call 1-800-873-8635 or visit www.morefreebooks.com.

* Terms and prices subject to change without notice. Prices do not include applicable taxes. N.Y. residents add applicable sales tax. Canadian residents will be charged applicable provincial taxes and GST. Offer not valid in Quebec. This offer is limited to one order per household. All orders subject to approval. Credit or debit balances in a customer's account(s) may be offset by any other outstanding balance owed by or to the customer. Please allow 4 to 6 weeks for delivery. Offer available while quantities last.

Your Privacy: Silhouette is committed to protecting your privacy. Our Privacy Policy is available online at www.eHarlequin.com or upon request from the Reader Service. From time to time we make our lists of customers available to reputable third parties who may have a product or service of interest to you. If you would prefer we not share your name and address, please check here. ☐

Help us get it right—We strive for accurate, respectful and relevant communications. To clarify or modify your communication preferences, visit us at www.ReaderService.com/consumerchoice.

HARLEQUIN®

A Romance

FOR EVERY MOOD™

Spotlight on

Classic

Quintessential, modern love stories
that are romance at its finest.

See the next page
to enjoy a sneak peek from
the Harlequin® Romance series.

See below for a sneak peek from our classic
Harlequin® Romance® line.

Introducing DADDY BY CHRISTMAS by Patricia Thayer.

MIA caught sight of Jarrett when he walked into the open lobby. It was hard not to notice the man. In a charcoal business suit with a crisp white shirt and striped tie covered by a dark trench coat, he looked more Wall Street than small-town Colorado.

Mia couldn't blame him for keeping his distance. He was probably tired of taking care of her.

Besides, why would a man like Jarrett McKane be interested in her? Why would he want to take on a woman expecting a baby? Yet he'd done so many things for her. He'd been there when she'd needed him most. How could she not care about a man like that?

Heart pounding in her ears, she walked up behind him. Jarrett turned to face her. "Did you get enough sleep last night?"

"Yes, thanks to you," she said, wondering if he'd thought about their kiss. Her gaze went to his mouth, then she quickly glanced away. "And thank you for not bringing up my meltdown."

Jarrett couldn't stop looking at Mia. Blue was definitely her color, bringing out the richness of her eyes.

"What meltdown?" he said, trying hard to focus on what she was saying. "You were just exhausted from lack of sleep and worried about your baby."

He couldn't help remembering how, during the night, he'd kept going in to watch her sleep. How strange was that? "I hope you got enough rest."

She nodded. "Plenty. And you're a good neighbor for

coming to my rescue."

He tensed. Neighbor? *What neighbor kisses you like I did?* "That's me, just the full-service landlord," he said, trying to keep the sarcasm out of his voice. He started to leave, but she put her hand on his arm.

"Jarrett, what I meant was you went beyond helping me." Her eyes searched his face. "I've asked far too much of you."

"Did you hear me complain?"

She shook her head. "You should. I feel like I've taken advantage."

"Like I said, I haven't minded."

"And I'm grateful for everything…"

Grasping her hand on his arm, Jarrett leaned forward. The memory of last night's kiss had him aching for another. "I didn't do it for your gratitude, Mia."

Gorgeous tycoon Jarrett McKane has never believed in Christmas—but he can't help being drawn to soon-to-be-mom Mia Saunders! Christmases past were spent alone…and now Jarrett may just have a fairy-tale ending for all his Christmases future!

Available December 2010,
only from Harlequin® Romance®.

HREXP1210

Silhouette *Desire*

USA TODAY bestselling authors

MAUREEN CHILD

and

SANDRA HYATT

UNDER THE MILLIONAIRE'S MISTLETOE

Just when these leading men thought they had it all figured out, they quickly learn their hearts have made other plans. Two passionate stories about love, longing and the infinite possibilities of kissing under the mistletoe.

Available December wherever you buy books.

Always Powerful, Passionate and Provocative.

Visit Silhouette Books at www.eHarlequin.com

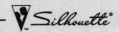

SPECIAL EDITION

USA TODAY BESTSELLING AUTHOR

MARIE FERRARELLA

BRINGS YOU ANOTHER
HEARTWARMING STORY FROM

When Lilli McCall disappeared on him
after he proposed, Kullen Manetti swore
never to fall in love again. Eight years later
Lilli is back in his life, threatening to break
down all the walls he's put up to
safeguard his heart.

UNWRAPPING
THE PLAYBOY

*Available December
wherever books are sold.*